Murderous Affections

Murderous Affections

Lousie Murphy Gearin

All rights reserved. No part of this book shall be reproduced or transmitted in any form or by any means, electronic, mechanical, magnetic, photographic including photocopying, recording or by any information storage and retrieval system, without prior written permission of the publisher. No patent liability is assumed with respect to the use of the information contained herein. Although every precaution has been taken in the preparation of this book, the publisher and author assume no responsibility for errors or omissions. Neither is any liability assumed for damages resulting from the use of the information contained herein.

Copyright © 2012 by Lousie Murphy Gearin

ISBN 978-0-7414-7276-2

Printed in the United States of America

This is a work of fiction. Names, characters, places, and incidents either are the product of the author's imagination or are used fictitiously. Any resemblance to actual events or locales or persons, living or dead, is entirely coincidental.

Published February 2012

INFINITY PUBLISHING
1094 New DeHaven Street, Suite 100
West Conshohocken, PA 19428-2713
Toll-free (877) BUY BOOK
Local Phone (610) 941-9999
Fax (610) 941-9959
Info@buybooksontheweb.com
www.buybooksontheweb.com

This Novel is Dedicated to:

My son Dr. Richard Spring, a clinical psychologist and musician, who edited the manuscript of this book.

My Son and daughter-in-law Stephen and Cindy Spring, licensed clinical social workers, and green-thumb growers of great gardens of flowers and vegetables, who bring our family together for feasts on holidays

My daughter, Ginger Gearin, recreation therapist, and skilled proof reader, who walks in the door wanting to read anything I write.

My husband, Gordon Gearin, who always supports my efforts and without whom I could not manage book signings.

Chapter One

Clarence Stembridge shifted his hefty body, moving his rocker closer to the fireplace. He leaned forward and tapped his pipe on an ashtray. The luxuriously decorated brown den with touches of red and gold was cozy. Outside, however, the temperature had dropped to near freezing and two inches of snow covered the ground. Clarence's radio on the nearby table and a television across the room both portrayed...at high volume...the exciting results of winning plays of two of his favorite teams. He was a happy man, completely unaware of the dark figure coming up behind him.

Hours later; April, his pretty young wife found him bludgeoned to death. She gasped in horror, grabbed the telephone and called police. Only moments later she realized she could not account for her time away from home, and their odd marriage was already in question in the minds of many people.

***

Yellow crime scene tape circled the Southern mansion with white Corinthian columns. The winter snow revealed shoe prints near a broken back window. The eager Columbus police made casts. Fingerprints were taken, but Police Chief Joseph Hillman knew this was just the beginning. Whose prints? The medium sized, southern city of Columbus, Mississippi, had been largely populated with long-time residents and their descendents for many years. Now, however, truckers with huge transport vehicles, a thriving college and a military base had altered the old city's population. Still, Hillman was a determined man who had once solved the murder of a prominent politician who had many enemies. "Details," he often said, "look for the sneaky, hiding little details."

Inside the mansion, April Stembridge stayed as long as she thought might be reasonable in the upstairs bathroom. What on earth could she say when questioned? She sat at the vanity and shook her head. No use putting it off. She'd simply have to lie, and she trembled at the thought! She knew she didn't lie well, but she'd have to try. Too much was at stake for the truth. It wasn't that she hadn't cared for Clarence. She had in a grateful kind of way, but she was not crying. Oh, better do something about that! She washed her face purposefully getting soap in her eyes to make them red. *Remove all the make-up, too.* Now she looked pale except for the sprinkle of freckles across her nose that came naturally with her auburn hair.

A knock at the door and April knew it was time to face the detectives. "Ma'am," the young albino maid said, "They're waiting for you and getting sort of impatient."

"Thanks, Mary Jean," April said, "I'll be right down." April remembered Mary Jean had seen her leave and return, but she appeared not to make anything of it. Still, the girl would be questioned, so April was glad she had not claimed to be at home.

Moments later April descended the spiral staircase to face the detectives and the swarm of other officers working in the mansion.

A young detective spoke. "Mrs. Stembridge?"

"Yes, I'm April Stembridge," she said. She stepped down the last two steps and into the foyer.

"I'm Detective John Kelly. I believe you spoke with Captain Hillman earlier."

"Yes, on the telephone," April said.

"I'm sorry to have to question you at this time, but it's necessary. We need to collects facts as soon as possible. Time matters greatly in these situations."

"I understand," April said. "Let's go in the parlor." She gestured. "To your right."

"After you Miss ... excuse me, Ma'am."

April smiled. Did she really look so unattached? Well, she was only nineteen and Clarence was forty-seven.

The parlor furnished with antiques offered two chairs, close together by a table. April suggested they sit there. *I have to appear co-operative. Just don't let him ask me the wrong questions!*

"I believe you said you were not at home when the murder occurred," Detective Kelly said. April noticed that he was quite handsome with dark hair and blue eyes. She observed also that he appeared a bit shy ... intimidated somehow, with his head tipped and a downcast glance or was it that he felt attracted to her?

"That's correct," she said with a handkerchief clasped in her hands.

"You are such a lovely young lady. People must wonder," he said smiling.

"Yes, but they don't understand," she said and relaxed.

"Outsiders misjudge you, you think?" he asked.

"Some do, yes," she said. *He seems more a counselor than a detective.*

"In what way?"

"They sometimes think I married Clarence only for his money," April said.

"Where exactly were you tonight?" he asked. His tone was firm, professional. He looked at her directly with steady blue eyes.

Oh! I'm in trouble! He's neither intimidated nor attracted. That shy act must have been intended to throw me off guard.

"You did hear my question, didn't you, Mrs. Stembridge?"

"Uh, yes. I...well, I took a long drive. I was upset. Clarence loves to drown in those..." She started to say 'awful' but decided not to use that word in case he was also a football lover. She finished with, "those football games. He plays them so loud it gets on my nerves and we argued." She put the handkerchief to her eyes and held it there for a long moment. A lie. There'd been no argument.

"So you argued? What did you say?"

"I...I'm sorry now I argued. Poor Clarence, I never wanted him hurt. I know some people made fun of him, but he was really a good man."

"Made fun of him?"

"Yes. I thought you probably knew that. He was injured in an automobile accident when he was in college and it...according to his sister, Claudine, made him become a bit of a cripple both physically and mentally."

"But you married him anyway."

"He was kind. I did not grow up in a good home," April said. She felt better now that she could speak some truth. The long drive in the car was definitely not true unless one considered ten miles a long drive.

"He is also quite wealthy," Kelly said. "I imagine that had some influence."

"Somewhat. Of course, everyone likes a beautiful home and money," she said. Again the truth.

"But pretty young wives sometimes want an inheritance from an older man. Was that your motive in getting rid of him?"

April stood. "I did nothing to get rid of him! Don't accuse me."

"Sit down, Ma'am. We're not finished."

April sat. "So what else do you wish to accuse me of?"

"A lover, perhaps?"

"My husband is...was my lover," she said and to her surprise tears came to her eyes.

"Very well. That's all for now," Detective Kelly said. "We'll talk again."

April stood and felt herself trembling. She dreaded ever seeing Kelly again. She was afraid he was more, much more than he appeared on the surface.

***

April knew about sneaky personalities. Otherwise, her life would have been different. How many times had her father come on as loving and then found a way to bore into her child's heart with criticism? Not that he had ever stopped doing it now that she was an adult. Studying psychology at the library, she came across a word that fit him. Sadistic. Oh, not that he beat her. He didn't. It was a mind game that amused him. Was handsome, young detective Kelly like that? She knew she had a weakness for handsome men, but this one scared her. Besides, she was not in the market.

On her birthday, the 12th of March, she'd left Watsonville for Columbus and found the "girl Friday" job at Stembridge's Antiques. Great luck on her very first day in town. The second day, in a chance encounter at a café, she'd met Mitchell Redmond, Air Force Captain Mitchell Redmond, and fell crazy in love. She thought her lousy world had turned from upside down to wonderful at last. But now this horrible murder had her deeply shaken.

Mitchell!

Oh, she must be losing her mind. Mitchell would need to know! She reached for the telephone but quickly replaced the receiver. What was she thinking? She couldn't call him. The police undoubtedly had tapped the telephone. Maybe just a note to warn him to keep quiet. No! Nothing in writing. She thought of the officer's club where they'd been earlier. Now she wished they'd not gone there for dinner. They should simply have stayed at the motel where they'd been so careful not to be seen by outsiders. She dropped her head in her hands. She would have to force herself to stay away from Mitchell until this terrible event ended. No way, however, could she keep Mitchell from contacting her. What would she say? If only he'd hear the news before he called.

Claudine!

She'd forgotten! Claudine didn't know Clarence was dead! She would be flying in within the hour from Ireland, where she'd gone on a buying trip. At least the chauffer would be meeting her. Thank Heaven! The first word wouldn't have to come from her lips.

April knew Clarence's body was now with the coroner. The shock of finding him so horribly dead made her tremble each time she remembered. She'd felt tenderness toward him. He was so unlike her father. He'd treated her as gently as he did his pet kitten, Jamie Sue. He even started calling her "Kitten." She smiled remembering that.

Of course, Clarence was not handsome and she'd found out quickly that if Claudine hadn't operated the antique business, he would have lost it. Mostly he ran the cash register and enjoyed talking with customers, but he was not smart. He was, however, a gentle giant, and much to her surprise, not a bad lover, not that she was all that experienced to make comparisons. Maybe before the accident he'd been right on track with being normal or even bright. But she knew his kindness was not what led her to marry him. Would she have done that if she'd never met Mitchell Redmond?

April heard the car enter the garage at ten thirty and ran to meet Claudine. Within moments they were in each other's arms. Tears coursed down Claudine's wrinkled cheeks.

"Who could have possibly wanted to murder our precious Clarence?" Claudine cried.

"I don't know. I don't know," April said. "He was so gentle ... so good."

Claudine stood back from the embrace. "Whoever did it will pay and pay in a most painful way! I'll make certain of that," Claudine said. Her voice was so firm and threatening that for a moment April felt it was directed at her. Surely not! They were close, weren't they? Claudine had even proposed their marriage. She wanted April to be there for Clarence when she was gone, and hopefully to bear a child, so they'd have an heir.

April spoke softly. "Claudine, he...he had no enemies. I don't understand."

Before responding Claudine turned to the chauffer. "Take my luggage on in, Jayson, and let's go in, too, April. Let's sit at the kitchen table and talk this over. I could use some coffee," Claudine said.

As they left the garage and walked into the house, Claudine said, "You know my nephew...our reckless nephew, Dell, wants in the business. To take over when I'm gone. Well, he's not going to! Dell Stembridge is a loser. You know he's been heavily into gambling. Such a spoiled young man! He has never assumed any responsibility for his behavior. Oh, no! He feels the world owes him everything, and he owes nothing."

"I know," April said, not that she really knew, but she'd heard Claudine speak of him before.

"I'm not saying he's the killer, but I'll have my eyes on him," Claudine said. "He's on the list I thought of coming in from the airport."

April said nothing, but she thought people with gambling debts could become desperate. She shivered. She'd never liked the way Dell Stembridge looked at her. Could she be next on his list if it served him right somehow?

In the spacious, totally modern kitchen, April and Claudine sat in a corner breakfast nook overlooking a flower garden that was covered in the winterkill of dead plants. April looked at it for a moment in the floodlights and considered the darkness of death, but the perennial plants would live again. Hopefully, Clarence would as well, in a heavenly rebirth. Tears sprang to her eyes. This time her tears came not just over the sadness of his death but over her guilt in deceiving him as well. She had made her conscience passably satisfied by being especially good to Clarence, but the sense of betrayal was there, and it wouldn't go away.

Claudine started to pour the coffee from an always-ready coffee pot. April sometimes worried about what all that coffee drinking might be doing to Claudine's health. How on earth would she be able to operate the antique store if Claudine died? She felt a genuine fondness and appreciation for her fifty-six-year-old sister-in-law, but she also needed her guidance.

"I think I'll have milk instead," April said. "My stomach feels a little queasy."

"Oh, no wonder, dear. With all this and the fact that you're pregnant as well. How sad Clarence will never see his child, but at least he had the thrill of knowing he would be a father. You know how he loved his "Kitten." He would have been a loving father. I'm sure of that."

"I'm sure he would have," April said.

"Thankfully, you're going to keep our family name and the business going. April, I must begin to teach you more about it. Oh, but my poor brother! I'll miss him so! Every day for the rest of my life I'll miss my sweet brother. We were close as children, and it never changed even after he...after his terrible accident."

April shook her head. "This is such a horrible mystery. How could he be killed without a single enemy?" April said.

"People kill for all kinds of reasons. Money and power are the main reasons, I think," Claudine said.

"But who would benefit from his death? You operate the business," April said.

"There are people who would hope to benefit. I made a mental list on the way in from the airport. Besides, our nephew, I thought of Matton. Matton Lennet has wanted to buy us out for years, and he's a lousy, cheating crook. While he knew Clarence didn't run the business, he'd might think I'd give it up...might move away when I no longer needed to consider Clarence. You know Clarence loved coming to work every day, and Matton darn well knew that."

"He was in the store yesterday morning talking to Clarence, but I don't know what he said. Clarence didn't appear to be really upset, although I saw him frown several times. I think Matton liked to tease him, and now I wish I'd walked over there."

Claudine wiped away sudden tears before continuing. "I thought of that street person who came by begging last week," Claudine said. "He was a big guy and very demanding. Jayson said Clarence gave him money. Five dollars. Even so the creep swung his fist at Clarence. If Jayson hadn't been there to rush the man out, who knows what would have happened? Jayson thought he was high on drugs."

"He wanted a lot more money and was really yelling at Clarence." April said, "Oh, I meant to tell you the detectives made casts of shoe prints in the snow outside the window," April said.

"Good! At least a beginning," Claudine said.

The telephone rang. Claudine was closer and answered it. "Yes. Yes, she's here. Just a moment." Claudine handed April the phone.

Oh don't let that be Mitchell! April thought.

April recognized the voice immediately. Aero's bad cold still made his voice sound raspy.

"April, anything I can do? Just heard on the news about your dad," Aero said.

"My husband," April corrected. "No, nothing you can do, but thanks."

"Your husband? Does Mitchell know?"

"I'm sorry...please, I need to hang up." April replaced the receiver still hearing Aero speaking on the line. Now what would the police make of that call if they were indeed listening?

"Who was that?" Claudine asked.

"Oh, some man who was a friend-of-a-friend I knew earlier," April said.

"The news is out, of course," Claudine said. "I'm sure we'll have many more calls and friends coming in by morning."

The detective stood in the doorway. "Excuse me, ladies. Miss Stembridge, I'm Detective John Kelly. I understand you've just arrived from Ireland. I hate to..."

"I am more than willing to talk with you, Detective, please join us," Claudine said gesturing to an empty chair.

"Just you, Miss Stembridge."

Claudine frowned.

"We've already talked," April said and left the kitchen.

Detective Kelly said, "First, let me express my sympathy. I'm sorry to need to question you now, but I need a few minutes of your time."

"Don't be sorry, Detective. I understand the importance and I want to help in any way I can. My brother was very dear to me and I mean to do everything in my power to see his murderer caught."

"Very well, then," Kelly said. "Suppose we start with questions about the people in your household. I understand you have two servants, a maid and a chauffeur. Anyone else besides your sister-in-law?"

"No. Well, yes, we have a couple of men who keep the grounds. Sam and Gregory Noble. They're rather old men, brothers, and appear very gentle."

"Where do they live?" Kelly asked.

"Just at the edge of our property in a small house we built for them and their much younger half brother, Lesley. Lesley is a body builder at a local gym. Actually, I haven't seen him in months. But then, I've had no occasion to do so."

"What are the approximate ages of the brothers?"

"Sam and Gregory must be in their late sixties. Lesley is twenty-nine. They celebrated a birthday for him last fall is why I know," Claudine said.

"Has there been any conflict with Clarence or you?"

"No. None. I don't think they're likely to be involved. However, I understand you must look at everything."

"Yes," Kelly said, "which leads me to questions about your young, very pretty sister-in-law. Why, and I hate asking this question...why would such a young woman choose to marry someone like your brother?"

Claudine bristled but then sighed and responded. "She's a lovely girl but she came from a poor, dysfunctional family. She and Clarence worked well together and seemed to really like each other. I saw an opportunity to accomplish a goal of mine. You see, neither Clarence nor I had married and therefore were without an heir. After a month of seeing how smart and sweet she is, I asked April if she would be willing to marry Clarence and become pregnant."

"You, not Clarence, made the proposal?" Kelly asked.

"Yes. At first, April seemed surprised and politely declined, but apparently she thought it over and came to me a few days later and agreed. We had a small wedding at her mother's church in Watsonville."

"And that was when?"

"The next week. Right away. I saw no reason to postpone it...the wedding I mean," Claudine said.

"And she became pregnant right away?"

"Yes, almost immediately."

"She doesn't look pregnant," Kelly said.

"I know, but tests reveal that she is," Claudine said.

"So she made a business deal," Kelly said.

Claudine sat upright. "I really find that offensive, Detective. I trust April completely. She's done nothing but be lovely to both Clarence and me."

"She said they argued tonight over his noisy football games," Kelly said. "Did she tell you she wasn't here when he was murdered?"

Claudine frowned. She appeared stunned. "She wasn't here? You know the house is so big. I thought she was in another area at the time."

"She said she went for a long drive after they argued. What do you think of that?"

"I don't know," Claudine said. She spoke softly and tears welled up in her eyes. Had she been fooled? Had she set up Clarence for murder?

"Perhaps, it was just as she said. Couples do argue at times and they tell me pregnant women can be temperamental," Kelly said. He rose from his seat with a smile, having planted just the seed he meant to drop.

Chapter Two

Two miles down the highway from the Air Base was Hector's, a favorite spot for the airmen and other young people. Eight years before Hector Mackie bought the building, it had been an old fashioned wooden store with a porch that stretched across the entire front. Having always been fascinated by the old west, Hector made repairs and decorated the building in a historic western theme. A small band played on weekends, and Hector, always dressed as a cowboy, did a little western comedy routine. Recently he added barbecue and beans to his menu of beer and soft drinks, and dropped hard liquor. A killing fight led to that decision. Though the changes helped, brawls and fist fighting continued to erupt from time to time, so he hired former boxer, Aero Laston, as bouncer.

***

Aero let the heavy wooden door slam as he walked into the nightclub. A tight, white t-shirt revealed his barrel chest and a hook tattoo on his right arm. Although the door closing was noisy, the clunky sound could barely be heard above the music and noise of the crowd.

Aero looked over the shadowy room, raking thick fingers through his bleached blond crew cut. He hoped to see Mitchell but didn't see him. Instead he saw his girl friend, Helen Madison. She waved vigorously at him from across the room, but he was not interested in seeing her. Not tonight. Nevertheless, Helen, a straw thin brunette, made her way through the crowd and took hold of his bare arm.

"Hi, Sweetie," she said grinning up at him.

He felt irritated but spoke in a calm, if raspy voice. "You seen Mitchell?" he asked, giving her very thin butt a double pat.

"Yeah. He was here, but you know Mitchell," she said, "always surrounded by women. Damn if he ain't good looking!

George Clooney would be no competition. I could go for him myself, except I got big, handsome you."

"Yeah. Yeah, sure." he said.

"I know you're big buddies, Aero, but defending him against jealous husbands and boy friends could get you killed. Even little guys carry guns. Honey, I just think you carry the 'like Jimbo' too far.

"Don't say that!" Aero said. "Don't you ever take down Jimbo."

"Oh, I wasn't doing that. I wasn't."

He gave her a half-gentle shove. "Go," he said.

Helen regained her balance. "I'm only thinking of you, Aero," she said but she left him and returned to the table where her friends were.

Aero continued through the crowd. He was glad for the darkness in the room. He couldn't allow his tears to be seen. Just Jimbo's name after five months brought back the guilt. There was no way to escape the fact he'd killed his brother.

Well, it had made a sober man out of him. He'd never drink another drop of booze again…ever. Not just for the drunk driving problem, but to deny himself one of his real pleasures. He even loved the aroma of Old Charter.

Hector said, "Man, take a little drink now and then. It was an accident. You didn't mean to kill him." Hector didn't know it was more than that. He'd been jealous as hell of Jimbo from day one. Even as a four-year-old, he'd wished the newborn would die.

Their mother laughingly told everybody Aero had asked her if it was too late to send the baby back. He'd stood by, feeling worthless and ugly while everybody exclaimed over how beautiful, how smart, how altogether adorable James Henry "Jimbo" Laston was. Maybe it was natural to feel jealous, but not the way he'd taken it on as Jimbo grew. In secret, he hit the kid, sat on him many times until Jimbo could hardly breathe and even dipped his toothbrush in the commode. In their recent years, they'd had some good moments, but only because Jimbo made it happen...then came the car wreck.

Of course, Aero knew Mitchell was not Jimbo, but the first time he saw him it was like Jimbo had come back alive. The physical resemblance was incredible! He'd had to restrain himself from racing to embrace the guy. What a scene that would have made. He knew it was of no help to Jimbo to cater to Mitchell, but it gave him a kind of peace. Helen couldn't understand that. He'd never be able to explain it to her, but he was damned tired of her trying to talk him away from Mitchell. Sure, he knew envious little guys could carry guns and Sam Shecky in particular seemed very threatening. Aero had warned Mitchell about giving Shecky's woman too much attention...in fact, any attention, but Mitchell was into being adored. Now he saw him...laughing with Shecky's little blonde.

***

April opened the door to Dell Stembridge. He looked directly at her with that hostile expression she'd come to expect...and then beyond her. "Where's Aunt Claudine?" he asked.

"At the funeral home," April said.

"I see you're not wearing black," Dell said. He smirked. Although he bore a physical resemblance to Clarence and Claudine, having the same round, blue eyes and straight eyebrows, Clarence had been much better looking in his college photographs.

"What do you want, Dell?"

"Told you. I want to see Aunt Claudine. She's going to need help and I'm going to make her an offer she'll damn well take."

"You can wait in the parlor if you like," April said. She closed the front door.

"Don't dismiss me, little Miss Opportunist," he said, "You're not going to take over here."

"Like I said, the parlor is to your right," April said and turned to go.

Dell grabbed her arm, folded her in an embrace and kissed her hard on her mouth.

She jerked away and wiped her mouth with the back of her hand. "Yuck!" she cried. "You bastard! Leave me alone."

He grabbed her again. She kicked his shin hard. He yelled and grabbed his leg, recovered somewhat, and struck at her with his fist.

She dodged and screamed at him. "Don't you ever touch me again...ever!"

Mary Jean came running from the kitchen. "What's the matter, Mrs. Stembridge?" she asked. She carried a large, barbecue fork in her hand.

"Nothing that concerns you, Albino," Dell snapped, moving to grab the fork, but missing. Mary Jean circled his hand with it and then held it apart.

April was amazed and impressed with the girl's agility and bravery. She also thought it funny and laughed.

The back doorbell chimed.

"That's Claudine and Jayson," April said. She rushed to greet them followed by a limping Dell and Mary Jean, who still gripped the big fork.

Dell caught up with April. "You're going to be damned sorry. I promise you that. Nobody messes with this Stembridge and gets away with it," he said thumping his chest.

***

Alone at last, after refusing Dell's offer, Claudine bathed her face and studied her reflection in the mirror. How soon would her impending death show? So far she thought she still looked normal, but terminal cancer would change that in time. She still felt relatively well, and the sad ordeal of telling Clarence no longer faced her.

She had put off telling April as well, and now she wondered about her will. Now that Clarence was gone, she meant to make April and Clarence's child her sole heirs. But after the meeting with Detective Kelly she was troubled. Should she make the unborn child the only heir? Could one even do that? Surely April had nothing to do with Clarence's murder, but where was she when it occurred? She would ask her face-to-face and right now! She patted her damp face with a towel, left the bathroom and went to April's bedroom.

When April answered her knock, Claudine saw she looked pale and troubled. Still she had to have an answer.

"Come in," April said. She put an arm around Claudine. "This is terrible. I'm so sorry,"

"I want to talk with you," Claudine said. "Please, be honest with me."

"What is it? What's...? April shuddered. *Did Claudine know something?*

"I want to know where you were when...when he was murdered."

April trembled. "I...I'm so sorry. Now I wish with all my heart I had stayed here."

"Where did you go?"

April swallowed. *Oh, this lying!* "Driving. Just driving out into the night. Oh, Claudine, you don't know how much I wish I'd never left this house."

April's obvious emotional distress touched Claudine. Most likely she'd put too much weight on the young detective's suggestion. She folded April in her matronly arms. "Don't be too sorry, dear. Had you been here, you might have been murdered, too."

April broke into uncontrollable sobs.

Claudine kissed her head. "Don't keep blaming yourself. You didn't know."

Still shaking with sobs, April said, "I love you, Claudine." Claudine said, "I love you, too." She released April and spoke softly. "Try to get some sleep. We'll talk again tomorrow. We have so much facing us."

***

When April entered the breakfast room next morning, she motioned to Mary Jean to come forward.

"Yes, Mrs. Stembridge. What can I do for you?" the maid asked.

"I want to thank you, Mary Jean, for coming to defend me yesterday. You were very brave, and, gee, so agile! Anyway, I know each time I've worn this gold bracelet you've admired it. I want you to have it."

Mary Jean's hand flew to her mouth. "Oh, that's real gold! It's too expensive."

"Not so much. Only twelve karats. You deserve more, but I know you like this one, so, here, take it. I want you to have it."

"Thank you ma'am. Thank you," the girl said taking the bracelet, holding it momentarily against her heart before slipping it onto her arm.

Claudine, who was sipping coffee, watched. When Mary Jean went to the kitchen for April's breakfast, Claudine asked, "What was that about?"

April explained the episode with Dell Stembridge.

"Oh," Claudine said, "he is just impossible. He came here thinking he could work me. He knows I've always admired the old family home. Thinking he could make his way into the business, he offered to let me have it as a half share in the antique business. I had to laugh. Yes, I love the old place, but it needs a lot of repairs and isn't worth anything like the price he places on it."

"I remember he said he had a deal you wouldn't turn down. Maybe not in those words, but meant that."

"He seems determined. Now he claims I bought my share of the business from his father too cheaply. True, Horace was ill and in financial difficulty, but he set the price. I didn't. I don't feel I owe Dell anything."

Mary Jean appeared with April's breakfast. "Your orange juice and oatmeal. Anything else I can get for you?"

"No, thanks. Everything else I need is on the table."

"Very well, ma'am," Mary Jean said and returned to the kitchen

After a brief silence, Claudine said, "I think we may be able to have the funeral by next Thursday. The police should be ready to release his body by then, though they don't seem to have any new information to share."

"Is there anything I can do, Claudine?"

"No. I've made the necessary arrangements. What you can do though, is go to the supermarket and pick up a few items. Would you do that?"

"Yes, of course."

"I'll give you a list," Claudine said. She took a sip of coffee. *Should I tell April now about myr illness?* She hungered for emotional support, but thought it too much of a burden for April just now. No. It would have to wait.

***

April drove to the supermarket preoccupied with her guilty thoughts. She meant to do everything she could to please Claudine. No matter how much effort it took she meant to learn everything about the business and work hard to make up as much as possible for her deceitfulness.

She parked the navy Mercedes Clarence had given her and walked into the busy supermarket. She didn't see him at first. Mitchell! What was he doing here? She grabbed a cart and pushed it down a far aisle. He would follow her, she knew. Her heart pounded. They must not be seen together! What could she do? Then she remembered the stacks of pet foods and many cases of soft drinks in a somewhat shadowy section in the very back of the store.

No sooner than she had shoved her cart to the most remote area of the pet food section than he appeared. He also pushed a cart and had even tossed a few items in it. At least he was making some effort to disguise his real purpose.

"April," he said. "I had to see you."

At once she was thrilled simply at the sight of him...overwhelmed by his nearness, as if every fiber of her being responded and erased everything else in her life.

Her voice came in short breaths. "How did you know I'd be here?"

"Chance...well, sort of...I've been by your house several times and hoped you'd come out. You did and I followed you here. I'm surprised you didn't see me."

"I was preoccupied." Tears came then.

"Darling," he said and took her in his arms.

She knew she should push him away, but couldn't bring herself to do so. She could give up everything and deny herself anything if she could be with him the rest of her life.

He stroked her hair gently and she looked up at him. He kissed her passionately.

"Hey, you're trembling," he said laughing softly. "Or is that me?"

"Maybe both of us," she said. "Oh, Mitchell, I love you so much!"

Footsteps and a squeaking cart separated them. An elderly woman approached.

"Young man," she said, "would you put one of these big bags of dog food in my cart? I shouldn't lift it. Heart problems." She laid a hand on her chest.

"Of course," Mitchell said. He lifted the ten-pound bag of food she indicated and placed it in her cart.

"Thanks," the old lady said. She smiled and pushed her cart back out into the main area of the market.

When the woman was gone, April said, "I have to respect Clarence's memory, but we can get married later. Then we'll be together for our baby."

Mitchell bristled slightly. "It's the wrong time, April. Anyway it's not a baby ... just an embryo. I told you Aero knows somebody who can take care of it for you. You need to quit putting it off."

"No! Why do you want to kill our baby?"

He sighed deeply, impatiently. "I told you. The time is not right! I can't deal with it now."

Tears slid down her cheeks. "I won't do it. Oh, Mitchell, you don't know how ... what I'm suffering ... the guilt. Clarence thought and Claudine believes the baby is Clarence's."

"You told me. Actually, I didn't think you'd go for the abortion. Look, you can have the baby and do just fine with all that money."

"You don't care about our baby?"

"Stop that! I would care but ... why don't you get it, April? Now is just the wrong time."

"Maybe it's not the wrong time for all your flirting with other women. Are you taking them to bed, too?"

He threw his hands in the air. "I've got to go," he said.

"I thought you loved me, Mitchell. You don't."

He stepped back and took her in his arms again and kissed her. "I do, sweetheart. The other women mean nothing...just playing. You're my beautiful best love."

She responded to his kiss wanting to believe him. As always, one look into his handsome face and those eyes and she weakened. She knew she couldn't put him out of her life...not yet anyway, although the one ounce of reason left in her told her she should.

She drove home thinking of how easily they'd related until now... never running out of conversation or affection. They'd talked of their earlier lives when both, in different parts of the country, had been all-A students in high school. He'd been the quarterback on his football team. She'd won debates. His best friend left for Colorado after high school to get into bull fighting. Her best friend, Tracy Regal, exceptionally tall and beautiful, went to Hollywood to try to break into the movies.

April still felt a tinge of jealousy in remembering how Mitchell seemed so interested in hearing all about Tracy. He wondered if Tracy would become a star and be rich and famous, and when she might come home. He wanted to see photographs of her.

April sighed. She'd not heard from Tracy in months. Remembering what a scatterbrained, daring girl Tracy was, April could see her barging into studios making some kind of exaggerated play. Would her beauty get her excused? Hired? April worried about her. When they'd been together, Tracy often said, "Hey, take a chance. Don't be so cautious, April Johnson!"

Tracy had tried to talk her into the two of them going to Hollywood. Now she wondered if declining was the right choice. People told her she was as beautiful as Tracy. She didn't think so. Probably Mitchell wouldn't think so either, if they ever met.

Chapter Three

Claudine met her at the door as she brought in the groceries. "Where did you go?" she asked. "I'd forgotten the sour cream so I sent Mary Jean to get it. She said she didn't see you anywhere."

April swallowed. What could she say? "I know I was gone longer than I meant to be." In searching for an excuse, she remembered she had a new card of stamps in her purse. "I went to the post office to buy stamps. I'm sorry, it was a problem"

"Stamps? I could use a couple if you don't mind," Claudine said.

April thought it was a test. She was glad the lie worked. *Was she getting good at lying after all?* Still, she hated it. Would the day ever come when she wouldn't need to lie? She prayerfully hoped so.

"Here," April said. She removed the stamps from her purse and handed them to Claudine.

***

The name on the rural mailbox in Watsonville was Marvelous Johnson, but most everybody called April's father "Vel." He'd been his parents' very late adored and only child. They'd named him Marvelous Cody Johnson, but they called him "Sugar Foot" most of their lives. The fact that they'd been poor didn't keep Marvelous from being totally spoiled. He was overly fed and fat, which set him up for teasing when he was a youngster. Not being able to defend himself too well, he early on started taking his frustrations out on younger kids. In short, he became a bully. At age forty-eight he still enjoyed making others bend to his will and suffer.

April's mother, Flaudie Mae, a small, homely woman, hustled about getting ready for their trip to Columbus. Vel kept rushing her to get dressed, take care of his needs, and try not to forget anything. Forgetting or failing to do anything would surely bring on harsh words or worse. Once he pushed her against the stove and caused a bad burn on her arm. He threatened to beat her, but he never did, apparently enjoying the mental abuse more than physical assaults.

When they finally climbed into the faded brown pickup, Vel gunned the motor and streaked off down the gravel road. Flaudie Mae wanted to ask him to slow down, to be careful, but she knew it would only make matters worse. He'd laugh and drive even faster, dart around over the road, and do a number of near misses with bridge railings. She sat with her hands folded and prayed.

***

The day of the funeral was bright but cold. April and Claudine were surrounded by friends, and Dell showed up to sit by them in the church. He was sober, neatly dressed and on his good behavior. April's parents, who had arrived late, sat in the back. April saw them and smiled weakly. Her father mouthed a kiss. Her mother returned the smile but appeared distressed. April understood why. She'd seen that look so many times. "Mama, leave him," April had pleaded, but Flaudie Mae was one of those women who was more afraid of the outside world than the miserable one she lived in.

About midway on the right side of the church, April saw the Police Chief Joseph Hillman, and two officers, including John Kelly. April wondered about their presence. Was it only out of respect, or did they have a motive? Ah, she remembered a movie once, where the murderer had a need to show up at the funeral. Had that happened here? Dell sat next to her, and she saw Matton Lennet, the other antique dealer, but no one else she recognized except the gardeners and their younger brother.

After the funeral and service at the cemetery, the sad-eyed Claudine clung to April's arm. "I hope the baby looks like him," she said. "You know the Stembridge's eyes are rather dominant."

April blinked. She hadn't considered that, but she knew offspring didn't always look like either parent. She was a prime example. She bore a strong resemblance to her maternal great grandmother, whose portrait hung on the living room wall at home.

Responding to Claudine's stated wish, April said, "I know. That would..." she couldn't say 'that would be wonderful.' No lie at Clarence's funeral! But Claudine seemed not to notice the unfinished sentence.

***

At Claudine's invitation, April's parents joined them for lunch at home. Friends and neighbors brought food and flowers, and some lingered to visit briefly. All visitors, however, soon left except one long-time friend of Claudine's. The two of them stood talking in undertones near the side door.

Vel heaped his plate and ate greedily, but Flaudie Mae, like April, ate only a small amount of food and sipped a little apple juice.

When her father left to go to the bathroom, April put an arm around her mother. "Are you alright, Mama?" she asked.

"About as usual, honey...You know how it is."

"I can help you, Mama," April said. "Would you like to move?"

"No. I can't see my way to do that."

"Why?"

"Vel needs me."

"Oh, Mama!"

"Well, honey, what you don't understand is, he's not always bad. Then, too, he'd follow me. Maybe things would even be worse. Sometimes there's even a killing."

Vel returned wiping his nose with his sleeve and coughing.

"I want you to think about it," April said. "Let me know if you change your mind," April said.

Vel took a seat at the table on the other side of April. "You lookin' mighty good Baby Girl," he said. "Prettiest gal at the funeral."

"Oh, Daddy, how I look is not important."

"Yes, it is. It got you all this," he gestured with his hand. "I reckon you're one smart cookie. Beauty and brains," he put an arm around her. "Now you can help your old dad out. The house needs paintin' and there's a few other things. Like I could use a new truck. I got my eye on a big black Ram I saw yesterday at the Dodge place."

"I'd have to talk that over with Claudine," April said.

"You mean you don't have your own bank account?"

"No," April said. *A lie.* "We have a joint account."

"Well, you need to change that, Baby Girl. Change that right away."

April smiled. *So you can get to me for money. No I'm not ready for that...not for you and I may never be.*

"You didn't answer me, April. Get that done this very week...no later than next week," he ordered.

"I don't know. We'll just have to see," April said.

Claudine's friend left and she came to the table.

"I hear April don't have her own bank account," Vel said to Claudine.

Claudine glanced at April and saw April bite her lip and shake her head slightly.

"Money matters take time," Claudine said. "April is well provided for, Mr. Johnson so you don't need to worry about her."

"She's grown and a widow," Vel said. "She may need to see a lawyer."

"No, Daddy. I won't see a lawyer."

"Maybe not right away, Baby Girl, but I'll come take you to one if need be," Vel said.

"Shouldn't we go now, Vel?" Flaudie Mae asked. "You know the cows are going to need milking."

"I'll let you know when we'll leave," Vel said.

"April," Claudine said, rising from her chair, "could I speak to you in the kitchen?"

"Of course."

"No need for secret talkin'," Vel said. "We'll go now, but April you do as Daddy says." He pointed a finger at her. "I'll check on you next week." He rose from his chair. "Come on, woman," he said to Flaudie Mae.

Flaudie Mae kissed April's cheek. "Bye Sweetheart," she whispered before quickly following Vel out the door back to the old brown pick up.

When they were gone Claudine said, "I saw your face. Obviously, you didn't want your father to know you had a bank account. You'll soon have more money, too, April. Clarence made a will leaving you his share of everything."

"I didn't know that," April said. Tears flooded her eyes.

"It's only right," Claudine said. "You may do as you choose about helping your parents. I know about them, of course, and I can see why you have a problem with your father. Surely, though, there must be something good about him."

"I don't know that you'd call it good, but he takes great care of his two hounds. I mean he feeds them well, kisses and pets them and takes them to the vet. I think he likes them because they're so devoted to him. He can control them, shout at them and even whip them, but they'll come crawling back."

"The nature of dogs," Claudine said.

"He's mean," April said. "I don't intend to give him a dime, but I'll do anything Mama will allow me do to help her."

"April, I don't quite know how you've turned out so well unless it was through your grandmother's help."

"Grandma lived next door, and she did a lot for me. I might still be in Watsonville, except Grandma died last year, and I just couldn't take it anymore. I was working as a waitress at a little café, and Daddy was taking my money, all except the tips I hid from him...which wasn't much."

"It was definitely time to leave," Claudine said. "I'm glad you did."

Tears flooded April's eyes.

"Why, what's wrong?" Claudine asked, and took April in her arms.

April shook her head. "I don't deserve all this," she said.

"Nonsense," Claudine said, "You do. Now dry your tears and let's both get some rest."

When they parted Claudine thought she would wait at least another week before she shared the doctor's message of her illness with April. "Three to six months," he'd told her. Would that give her enough time to prepare April to take over the business? Nineteen was so young! Still, April was bright and willing to learn. Claudine sighed. At least, an heir would be carrying on their legacy. That part probably would please her ancestors if they knew. Some believed that the beloved dead could see those left behind on earth. At this time she liked to think so.

***

Police Chief Joseph Hillman frowned as he sat at his desk. He closed a thin file. "We've made poor progress," he said to John Kelly. "About all we know is the shoe prints were bedroom slippers probably purchased at the dollar store. Big clue." He shook his head and laughed. "Ridiculous," he said.

"And we haven't found the shoes, but somebody in that file we have on all those suspects can still reveal something significant," the detective said.

"We hope, but we don't know that, John. I'd hoped for more progress."

"I still suspect that pretty young wife," Kelly said. "You know I have some experience in that area."

"Don't be too quick to draw conclusions. The fact that your father married a young woman and cut you out doesn't mean it happens every time."

"Maybe not, but I'm going to watch her like the proverbial hawk."

"Do you have any clues?" the chief asked.

"Not yet," Kelly said. "I asked Henry to do a stakeout, and all he can tell me so far is she went to a supermarket. He said he went inside but didn't see her until she checked out. Probably she went to the rest room."

"What about the nephew?"

"He's in debt big time. Can't seem to stay away from the casinos. Benny's been watching him," Kelly said. "And before you ask, sir, nothing on the other antique dealer."

The chief sighed. "We're doing all we can at the moment, but we need a break."

"We'll get one. I'm going back to talk with the pretty young widow," Kelly said rising from his seat.

"You seem mighty taken with her looks. Better watch it, she may get to you," Chief Hillman said.

"Not a chance," Kelly said, "It's just that I'm aware her looks are what put her there."

***

From her upstairs bedroom, April saw the detective leaving his parked car. *Now what? Does he know something else? Does he know about Mitchell?*

She dug her nails into the palms of her hands. *Calm down. Relax. Don't let him get you rattled.* She took a deep breath and prepared to greet him at the door.

She waited until he rang the doorbell before she opened the door. In a mirror near the door she glanced at her reflection and smiled to relax her face.

"Good morning, Detective," she said.

"Good morning, ma'am. May I have a word with you?"

"Certainly. Come in." She gestured with her hand. "You know where the parlor is."

When they were seated, as before, in the same two chairs by the small table, Kelly said, "When I was here before I didn't ask you about your friends. I'd like you to list them for me. Addresses and telephone numbers." He held a pen above a small notebook.

"I don't have all that information. I mean addresses and telephone numbers. When I first came to Columbus the girl at the bus station told me where I could get a room. It was in a home where she and two other girls boarded."

"And where was that?"

"On Fourth Street, but I don't remember the number. It's a brown Victorian house."

"I know the house," the detective said. "A widow Downey takes in girl boarders."

"Yes. She was kind to me. Let me stay without paying until I got my first check," April said.

"Who were the other girls?"

"I don't think they're still there. One of them was getting married and leaving soon after I arrived and I don't know what happened to her roommate. Their names were Joan Apton and Carnell Housong. My roommate was Susan Mason...the clerk at the bus station. She may still be there. We didn't become friends. I'm kind of a neatness freak and she...thought I was

silly about it. Still, we managed to make it for two months. Then, you know, I got married."
"You surely had dates. Who did you date?"
April swallowed. *Oh no! But I have to answer.* "I dated an Air Force captain. A pilot. He may no longer be at the air base."
"When did you see him the last time?"
"Gosh, you mean the date...I can't say. I can't even tell you what I had for lunch yesterday," April said.
"Don't joke. I'm serious, Mrs. Stembridge. Give me a date," the detective said.
"I'm sorry. I can't. Besides, what does it matter?"
Kelly set his lips in a fine line. "Well, let me put it this way...have you seen him since you married?"
"Yes. I saw him on the street one day. Now don't ask me for the date. I don't check my calendar every day."
"Have you been intimate with him?"
"No! Of course, not!" April said slamming her hand on the table. *A lie, but a pleasant one! I can't stand this damn detective!*
"Shouting is not necessary, Mrs. Stembridge. What is the captain's name?"
Oh, great now that! Well, Mitchell could handle it. "His name was Mitchell Redmond, but as I said, he may no longer be at the air base."
"His phone number?"
"I have no idea," April said. *Wow, a lie he could catch me in, but I guess I have to chance it.* Later she wished she'd said she didn't remember. Too late now.
"Other friends or dates?" he asked. "You know I can find out so you may as well tell me."
"No one else in Columbus," April said.
"And elsewhere?"

"Some in my hometown of Watsonville, but I haven't seen them for a while."

"Give me their names and addresses," Kelly said.

April sighed. She thought it pointless, but she listed them for him.

"Your hometown boyfriend was Lester Hill?"

"Yes, but I haven't seen him since I left Watsonville."

"Was he happy about your marriage?"

"Oh, for goodness sake, Detective. We weren't serious ... just went on a few fun dates. Lester was more interested in computers than anything else."

"And what did he do on the computer?"

"I don't know. Games and chat rooms I think."

"Very well, that's all for now," Kelly said.

"Good," April said, "I hope you find the murderer. I really want that person found and prosecuted."

"Um hum," Kelly said taking his leave.

When the front door closed, April panicked. What if Mitchell didn't handle the questioning well? *Oh, he's smart, he'll know what to say. Surely he will. But what if Aero is questioned?* Her heart pounded. She was afraid of John Kelly's apparent determination to find her guilty. *Wow! Damn those two other phone calls to Mitchell. Oh! Kelly will check that. What can I say? How could I explain them? At least I didn't call him the night of the murder. Thank heaven I didn't dial the number then! But there was Aero's call. How can I explain him? Better be prepared!*

Chapter Four

Detective Kelly made his way up the steps of the brown Victorian house. A girl of about eight years sat on the porch in a swing with floral pillows. "Hi!" she said. She was chewing gum and petting a black and white kitten.

"Is Mrs. Downey in?" the detective asked.

"Yes. She's cleaning up lunch."

"Thanks," Kelly said and rang the door chimes. "You must be Mrs. Downey's granddaughter."

"I am. I'm Judy," the child said. "I don't live here. I live in Alabama. You better ring the bell again. She don't hear too good."

"I see. Oh, here comes your grandmother," Kelly said when he saw the woman limping slightly as she came up the hallway.

"Oh, John, how are you?" Mrs. Downey asked.

"Fine. I see you're limping a bit."

"Arthritis," she said. "Oh, do come in or would you rather sit outside in the garden? Such a nice day."

"Yes, let's go to the garden," Kelly said. He walked with her to the side yard and opened the grilled iron gate to the garden.

When they were seated in chairs beside an umbrella table, he said, "I've come to ask you about a girl who boarded with you a couple of months ago. One named April."

"Oh, that was one problem girl! Always having men slip in her room. I finally had to ask her to leave. Since you grew up next door, you know that's not my way. The sexual revolution they call it. Phooey, it's a foolish thing for girls especially."

"So April was promiscuous?"

"April did you say? Oh, I thought you said 'Apton'. It was that Joan Apton who was so wild. Good heavens, I must get my hearing aids adjusted! Why that little April Johnson was the sweetest child. I was so sorry to learn of her husband's murder. Such a horrible thing! Do you have any idea who might have done it, John?"

Kelly sighed. *No help here. I'll try the air base next. Captain Mitchell Redmond here I come.*

"You didn't say," Mrs. Downey said. "Guess that's police secrets. Good to see you again, though, John. Come by anytime."

They walked together from the garden and she watched him enter his car and start the engine. They smiled and waved at each other. She remembered him as a cute little boy. Once he came to her when his parents weren't home. He must have been about five or six years old. She laughed remembering. He said a bug flew in his eye and wanted her to "get the bug guts out."

She entered the house remembering John's mother's illness and the young woman who nursed her until she died. Something wrong went on there. Hardly a month after the funeral, old man Kelly married that girl who must have been no more than twenty-two. Well, he didn't live long and off that girl went with a neat fortune. Moved to Hawaii somebody said.

***

Detective Kelly drove to the air base. At the entry gate he showed his identification and gave Captain Redmond's name. Kelly said he didn't know what squadron Redmond was in but needed to see him. The young military policeman wrote down information about the detective, and stepped inside his building for a short period of time. He returned shaking his head. "Captain Redmond is not available," he said.

"What do you mean, 'not available'" I showed you my credentials," Kelly said.

"He's not here. He's away on temporary duty," the military policeman said.

"On temporary duty. I see. When will he return?"

"In a few days perhaps. I was not given that information, sir."

"I'll be back," Kelly said and left.

He sped along the road toward Hector's nightclub. *That Aero person had some connection I'm sure of it. But what?* At the nightclub he saw only one old van. Daytime, but perhaps someone would be around. He parked his car and made his way to the front door.

After several pounding knocks on the door, Hector appeared. "Hello," he said. "What can I do for you, sir?"

"I'm detective John Kelly. I want to see Aero Laston, your bouncer, I believe."

"He's not here. Hasn't been feeling well and went into town to see a doctor," Hector said.

"What was his problem?"

"I'm not sure. Seems forgetful, and impatient ... says he's not sleeping more than a couple of hours at night. Can't seem to get over the death of his brother," Hector said. "Probably gone to get some sleeping pills."

"I see," Kelly said. "Do you know what connection he may have with an April Johnson?" Kelly asked.

"No. Well, he used to spend a little time with her and Captain Redmond when they came here," Hector said.

"Recently? Have they been here recently?"

"No. I haven't seen the young woman in sometime, although Captain Redmond is here pretty often."

"What is Redmond like?" Kelly asked.

"A real good looking guy apparently with a lot of charm. The women flock around him."

"April has not been here in recent times? Are you sure?"

"Yes. I understand she got married so I guess that's the reason," Hector said. "It was in the news that her husband was murdered."

"Yes, I know," Kelly said. "Thank you. I'll be back to see Mr. Laston another time."

"Is Aero in trouble?"

"I need to ask him a few questions," Kelly said.

"He's not being accused of anything?" Hector asked.

"No. Routine," Kelly said. "Routine."

"He's been very dependable on the job," Hector said.

Another burnt run, but the phone calls meant something. Next visit to April Stembridge. Let her explain the phone calls.

He slid into his car seat and hesitated. Better check in with the chief. He dialed the number and the secretary answered.

"Let me speak to the chief," Kelly said.

"He's not here, Detective. It seems there's been a drive-by shooting. A Miss Claudine Stembridge was hit."

"Who? What? Are you sure?"

"Miss Claudine Stembridge was shot."

"Was she killed? Where was she?"

"She was in her car on the road to the nursery. I don't know the extent of her injuries. Just happened about a half an hour ago."

***

April telephoned her mother. "Terrible news, Mama. Claudine was going to get some plants when someone shot her. We don't know who. I'm getting ready to go to the hospital to be with her."

"Oh, April, I'm afraid you're in danger! Maybe you should come home, honey."

"Our chauffer has volunteered to stay at the house to protect the maid and me. I don't think we're in danger, but Jayson thinks I could be."

"Are you at home now?" her mother asked.

"Yes, but I'm leaving now. Claudine is in surgery. Oh, Lord, I pray she's going to be all right, but I don't know."

"Your dad has been gone about an hour or more, coming to Columbus. You know he wants you to have your own bank account. I thought he'd be there by now, but he was going to stop and check on a tractor for sale."

"He'll just have to wait. I'm not dealing with anything about money now," April said. "Besides, the way he treats us, he doesn't deserve it."

"I know, honey. You don't have to give us anything," her mother said.

"Oh, Mama, don't say 'us,' I would...will give *you* anything you need."

"Well, give him something if you can, just to settle him down."

"I think if I start it, he'll just keep asking for more. I don't know what to do, but for now I'm not going to give him a dime!"

"He'll keep fussing. You know how he is."

"Let him fuss. If he wants money from me he's going to have to treat you better and I'll make that clear to him. Oh, the phone is ringing. Maybe that's news from surgery. Bye for now," April said. She pressed off her cell phone and rushed to pick up the land phone.

"Mrs. Stembridge," a nurse said on the phone, "you sister-in-law came through surgery just fine. Her head and shoulder wounds weren't as serious as we feared."

"Great! I'm on my way there now. Is she back in her room?"

"Not for a while. She's in recovery now, but she's doing well."

"Thank you so much!" April said. She hung up the receiver and sighed, but almost immediately remembered the crime. *Who wanted Claudine dead? And who might want to kill me as well?*

***

When Claudine awakened back in her hospital room, April kissed her forehead and said, "Thank God you're going to be all right."

Claudine whispered, "Thanks," and drifted off to sleep.

Later, awake but still drowsy, Claudine said, "I'm thankful I wasn't killed. I have unfinished business."

"This is so scary! I hope the police find him immediately," April said.

Claudine spoke in a determined voice. "I'm afraid for you, April. Call and have security installed at home... same company as at the store. I should've already done that."

"Jayson said he'd stay and protect us."

"He would try, but we need the security system."

"I'll take care of it," April said. "I'll call from here right now."

"Yes," Claudine said, and closed her eyes.

"I'll make the call and then be quiet," April said. "You need to rest."

***

At six o'clock in the evening, Dell Stembridge burst into the hospital room. "Aunt Claudine! Gawd! How in the hell are you? I heard you'd been shot."

April stood from her chair. "Not so loud, Dell, she's sleeping."

Claudine stirred and opened her eyes.

"Nope, she's awake," Dell said. He went to the bed, lifted Claudine's hand and kissed it. "So you got in the way of a bullet? Dang. Best avoid those things."

"Right," Claudine said, giving a weak laugh.

"Well, I thought I'd come see how I can help out. I could take over running the store for you while you're laid up "

"That won't be necessary, Dell. I'll be back at the store probably in a matter of days. In the meantime, it'll be closed."

"Oh, I doubt you'll mend that fast. Older folks don't mend so fast I hear," Dell said.

"I'm not that old. Besides, I can manage in a wheel chair and will direct April and Jayson. I mean to instruct both of them."

April said, "What happened to your forehead...and your hand, Dell? I see you're wearing bandages."

"Oh, that. I was cutting back shrubbery around the old home place and got scratched up a bit." He turned to Claudine. "I want you to see it when I get through, Aunt Claudine. You may decide you want it after all."

"No, I won't, Dell, but it's good you're fixing it up. Perhaps, you can sell it for a decent price and pay off your gambling debts. It might keep you from getting hurt."

"I'm not in that deep, and one of these days I could really hit the jackpot. I'm getting better at the game every day."

"Oh, Dell, I think you fool yourself," Claudine said. "I think you should get out of it and prepare yourself for a job."

"You mean, go back to college? Naw, not at my age."

"Plenty of people go back to college in their middle to late twenties and even older. Besides, there are other schools. The trade schools offer short courses of a year or two."

Dell stood rigid, hands on hips. "You really mean to cut me out of the antique business, don't you? I thought so, but I've tried to be reasonable and make you good offers."

April said, "Dell, please, you're upsetting her."

"I know she's been shot. Well, I'll tell you something Little Miss Opportunist, I feel I've been shot, too. But one day I mean to be in the business." He turned on his heel and left the room, slamming the door shut with a bang.

***

Police Chief Hillman called a meeting of his staff, including Detective Kelly and two Deputies, Carl Henry and Mason Carter.

"Let's hear any reports you have," the chief asked. "You first, John."

"I'm afraid I haven't much to go on. We know the gunshot that hit Miss Stembridge came from that small, dense wooded area not far from her home. I talked with the maid, Mary Jean Gearson. She was the only one home when I arrived."

"Where were the others? Where was Miss Claudine going?" the chief asked.

"The girl said Miss Claudine was driving herself to the nursery for some houseplants. She said April Stembridge was examining antiques and reading some material, trying to learn the business, and the chauffer was moving some furniture around."

"The maid was alone, though, when you arrived?" Hillman asked.

"Yes. I understand April Stembridge had left immediately for the hospital and the chauffeur was tending to Miss Stembridge's automobile by that time."

The chief tapped his pen on a notebook. "Who knew...or might have guessed Miss Claudine would be driving by that grove of trees near noon on that Friday?"

"It appears that only April, the chauffer and the maid knew, however, someone may have been watching for the opportunity," Kelly said. "Carl, you were the first to get to her after the shooting."

"Yes, I was close by. You know I'd been on stakeout in an effort to protect her since the murder. "Unfortunately, I couldn't prevent it or see who might have done it. It appears the shot came from the wooded area that she was passing."

Deputy Mason Carter interjected, "Adjacent to those woods, not far from the Stembridge mansion, there's the park with playground equipment for kids. Lots of people coming and going, and it's close enough to the road to observe traffic. Somebody could have checked on her from there."

"I really needed to be two people," Carl Henry said: one to attend her and another to search the woods immediately, although that might have resulted in another shooting."

"Did you check out the wooded area?" the chief asked.

"I did. I asked people at the play area if they'd seen anyone go into the woods or leave from there. Nobody claimed to see anyone, but they were watching their children. I walked into the woods and got scratched by some bushes. I saw some grass trampled down and searched for objects ... a cigarette butt or litter, any discarded items. Nothing."

"We have to try to look at motive, Carl. What have you noted about Miss Claudine's habits?" the chief asked

"I've observed she frequently drives down that road, and I've checked out where she might be going."

"And what did you find?" the captain asked.

"A place called Kayron's. It carries fancy imported foods and coffees. She went there once. On farther down is the nursery and next to it are the gardens where there's a tearoom that serves ladies lunch. She met another lady there once. Maybe more important though, is the health spa and beauty shop. Gets her hair done every Friday, and this was Friday."

"Since you've observed her, have you noticed anyone else who might have been doing the same?" Chief Hillon asked.

Carl Henry said. "There's a lot of traffic on that road. I haven't noticed anything in particular."

Chief Hillman put his hand on his forehead. "Could be most anybody then."

"I'm afraid so," Kelly said, "but I still have more digging to do. Haven't interviewed Dell Stembridge or that other antique dealer. Miss Claudine mentioned him as one who tried repeatedly to buy her out."

"You mean Matton Lennet?"

"Yes."

"Any information on either of those two men?" the chief asked.

"Matton Lennet's not a native. Hasn't been here a long time. He's had a couple of DUIs. That's all I know," Mason Carter said.

"I'm going to see Miss Claudine at the hospital next, and then I'll check out Dell Stembridge," Detective Kelly said. "Lennet's on my list, too. We'll surely get a break of some kind soon."

The chief again tapped the pen on his notebook. "This is very frustrating. See what you can find out and report back. We don't want this case to go cold on us."

Chapter Five

Detective Kelly decided to stop at the bus station on his way to interview Dell Stembridge. He hadn't remembered to ask Mrs. Downey about Susan Mason, but now he thought he should have. After all, she had been April's roommate. He sighed. He supposed being in Mrs. Downey's presence was so comforting he'd completely relaxed and failed to ask enough questions. For now, he'd interview the young woman if she could allow him the time from her job.

A lax time between bus schedules revealed an empty waiting area. Kelly spoke to the young woman behind the counter, "Miss Mason?"

"Yes. What can I do for you?"

"I'm Detective John Kelly," he said showing his credentials.

He noted Susan Mason had pretty blue eyes and a ready smile. She had, however, a large nose and almost no lips which kept the slender girl from being as attractive as she might otherwise have been. He wondered if she had been jealous of April, but he pushed that aside at the moment to hear what she had to say.

"Could we speak in private?" he asked. She nodded and motioned to a vacant waiting area in a corner where they might sit. No one else was around except a man in the office, using a computer.

As soon as they were seated, Kelly said, "I understand you had a roommate named April Johnson."

"Yes, I did. She was a neatnick who was always cleaning up. I like a more relaxed way...kinda throw my stuff around," she said and laughed.

"What about her dates?"

"She had this one boyfriend. A captain. She was completely, overboard crazy about him. He was amazingly good looking...really a little too pretty for my taste. I like a more rugged man. But that's beside the point, I didn't think he was as taken with her as she was with him."
"Why?"
"He didn't always call when he said he would and even failed to show up for dates a couple of times. That, even though she spent a night with him and a weekend when she said she was going home to Watsonville."
"Did Mrs. Downey know that?"
"No. April was always able to slip back in and I didn't tell on her. I thought she was making a fool of herself, but she was only nineteen and the captain was twenty-seven or eight, I think. I even wondered if he was married."
"Do you think he was?"
"Who knows? He came from somewhere out of state. Virginia or West Virginia, I think. He seemed to brag about being wealthy...showed pictures of a beautiful home, a lake and other scenery. She may have those pictures."
"You knew she married, I suppose," Kelly said.
"Yes. I think she could have been pregnant and married the older man so he would take care of her."
"Are you still in touch?"
"No."
"Thank you, Miss Mason. I'll see you again." He left promptly.
On the way to his car he decided he would visit April Stembridge again and take a look at the pictures of Redmond and his home. He felt certain she would still have them if she'd been so deeply in love as Susan Mason described.

He dialed the Stembridge residence and was told April had gone to visit her parents. In that case, he'd drive to the air base and check out Mitchell Redmond.

***

April wanted desperately to hear Mitchell's voice and to have some reassurance that he still loved her. She thought she should no longer be concerned about calling a former boyfriend, as the police would probably think of him now. Still, she decided to make the call on her cell phone rather than the land phone. As if it mattered, she finished dressing and put on makeup to look her best before dialing Mitchell's number. She so hoped he would be in although often he was not.

"Hello," Mitchell said in a pleasant voice, "Captain Redmond speaking."

"Oh, I'm so glad you're there," April cried, "I wanted so much to hear your voice. I've missed you terribly. How are you?"

"Fine," he said. "What do you want?"

"To talk with you, Mitchell. Why else? Did you not want to hear from me?"

"You know how I feel about...about things."

"I know. The time is not right, but maybe later. Maybe even a year or two. Oh, Mitchell, I love you so much. I can't think of my life without you."

"Stop it, April!" he said. "Stop it. I don't want to hear that."

April gasped and tears filled her eyes. "Mitchell," she said in a whisper.

"It's over," he said and hung up the phone.

She screamed, sobbed, paced the floor and wept until her eyes were red and puffy. *How could he break my heart after we've been so close? And his tone of voice! Oh, God. How could he hurt me so much?* In a sudden revelation, she realized she was like Mama after all! Loving Daddy even with his cruelty. It sobered her. The ounce of reason she had experienced before surfaced once again, and anger flooded her this time. *How dare he treat me so mean!* She went to her dresser drawer and took out the pictures he'd given her of himself and his fine home. She meant to rip them apart, but she held them for a moment and replaced them in the drawer. *Not yet. Maybe he'll call back. Maybe he'd had a bad day.*

She heard the doorbell. Mary Jean was not in, and Jayson was gone as well. She would have to answer the door...or maybe she'd ignore it. She went to the window and looked out front. It was that detective. Certainly she was in no mood to be hassled by him, but what if he had news? Maybe she should answer the door. She went to the bathroom and dabbed her eyes with a wet cloth. It helped only a little. The doorbell rang again. *Oh well, what does it matter if he sees I've been crying? He wouldn't know the real reason.*

She hurried down stairs and opened the door. Within seconds the security alarm started shrieking. She'd forgotten about it, but quickly punched in the code and stopped the noise. The telephone rang and she ran to grab it.

"Yes, I'm all right. Yes, 7898," she said.

Detective Kelly laughed. "Not used to the security system yet, I see."

"No."

"Good thing to have," he said, "but be careful who you reveal the coded messages to. I know them now, but they're safe with me."

"I should hope so."

"You could have them changed if you don't trust me," he said.

"With that I trust you," she said.

"But not otherwise?"

"You know where the parlor is. I'll be right with you. I have to reset the code."

"I'm not looking," he said, teasingly covering his eyes.

"Oh, go on," she said. *There he was being friendly again. What did he mean to try to trip her up on this time?*

When they were seated in the parlor, she asked, "Do you have any clues as to who killed my husband and tried to kill my sister-in-law?"

"You don't look well? Are you ill?" He asked.

"No. Forget how I look. The point is do you know who shot my sister-in-law?"

"We're working on it. Do you have any suspicions?"

"No. I have no idea who could have done this. I know Claudine gave you some leads to check out but I don't know."

"How about your boyfriend, Captain Redmond?"

"Oh, there you go! My former boyfriend. No, I'm sure he's not guilty."

"How do you know?"

"Well...I...just know he wouldn't."

"Go on, tell me how you know for sure."

"All right, I can't, but I think a better choice would be Dell Stembridge."

"I hear you were very much taken by the captain," Kelly said.

"So what? That has nothing to do with anything."

"Maybe more than dated," Kelly said.

"What business of yours is my dating?"

"Were you in love?" He asked while looking at her directly. "Really in love?"

Tears came to her eyes. *Oh, no!*

"I see," Kelly said, "and he wasn't always dependable I understand. Did it ever occur to you he might be married?"

April's eyes widened. "Married? No, never. Who has been telling you tales?" *Oh, no! He's talked with Susan. Darn her! Why did she have to blab!*

"Where is he from? Do you have his home address?" Kelly asked.

"I think it's Virginia or West Virginia, but no I had no reason to have his home address."

"I understand you have some pictures of his home. I'd like to see them."

"Why?" *Nobody else but Susan knew about the pictures. She was no friend for sure! Blab! Blab! Blab! When it was no business of hers!*

"Police business."

"I don't think it's police business. I think you're just nosey."

"Please. Just get the pictures."

"And if I don't?"

"You know I can get a search warrant." He said.

"Well, I think it's ridiculous. I don't know what good they'll be, but I'll get them." she said, and left to go upstairs.

A few minutes later when she laid the pictures before him, he looked at each one carefully, including the photograph of Mitchell Redmond. Had he been careful not to give her something as personal as a portrait?

"I'll take these with me now, but I'll return them later," Kelly said.

"I won't be here later. I'm going to the hospital to be with Claudine. You can leave them with the maid," April said, stood, and moved her chair back to end the interview.

Kelly stood also. "I hope you'll find Miss Claudine feeling better."

"Thanks. You know the way out," April said.

He laughed. "Forgot security again, huh? You'll have to take it off, let me out the door and reset it."

"Oh, very well, I'll tend to it. Goodbye," she said.

"This captain," Kelly said as they walked to the door, "...my advice...dry your tears." He walked out without looking back.

What did he mean? It sounded like caring, but probably was just another trick. April closed the door and reset the security system. She ran her hand over the small mound of her stomach. A little more than three months with six still to go.

***

When April arrived at the hospital, she found Claudine sitting up in bed with a notebook on her lap. She smiled and called, "Come on in!"

"You seem to be better today," April said. "That's great."

"I am better from my wounds, but I need to talk with you about...about some other matters." She sounded so serious, April immediately felt concerned. *What does she know?*

April sat in a chair across the room, but Claudine motioned for her to move close. "Bring your chair near the bed," Claudine said.

April drew the chair in close and waited.

"Are you all right?" Claudine asked. "You seem anxious."

"Yes, it's that detective. He keeps coming back, but he has no helpful information."

"Not knowing is frightening. I know you must be afraid. I'm sorry."

"I keep security on," April said, "and I pay attention to strangers when I'm out."

Claudine hesitated. "Close the door. What I have to say is private."

April did as she requested and returned to her chair. Her heart pounded. *This sounds serious.*

"My gunshot wounds are healing, but I have another problem, April. I have lung cancer. I never smoked and neither did Clarence, but we did use chemicals in restoring furniture at times. Oh, I don't know. That may not be it either. In any event, I have cancer."

"Cancer?" April frowned. "But surely the doctors can do something."

"I'm afraid not. I've been told I have from three to six months to live. That troubles me because I wanted to prepare you to carry on the business, and I wanted so much to see the baby."

"Can't you go somewhere...like some special treatment place?"

"I could and I may, but I think my time is limited. Actually, April, the business could be sold. It's been a sentimental thing for us in a way and we've enjoyed it, but our father, really our grandfather, is the one responsible for our wealth. He made investments that paid off handsomely."

"Your grandfather?"

"Yes. Years ago grandfather put money in Micheloud & Cie, a Swiss company, where we have a great deal of money. Locally, people consider us millionaires, but they don't know about our Swiss account. You and the baby will be quite wealthy. I've prepared everything with Hunter Warren, our lawyer."

"I haven't met him," April said.

"I know, but he knows all about you and he'll be over to meet you soon. He's aware of my condition." Claudine dropped her head briefly and then looked up again. "April," she said, "wealth is a good thing and a bad thing. Good because you can have most anything money can buy, but be very guarded in giving any information about your wealth. It could endanger your life. I don't want to frighten you, but if all that we have were known, someone could kidnap you and demand a ransom from me. Later, when I'm gone, if it were known, the baby could be in danger."

"Oh, Claudine! I don't know what to say. I don't deserve all this. I want you to live!"

"I expect to outlive the doctors' predictions, but I don't know. Anyway, let's talk about the baby. Have you thought of what to name him or her?"

"I thought of having that examination to see if it's a boy or a girl," April said.

"Amniocentesis? I'd rather you didn't. There's some risk I understand. Minor maybe, but no, let's just wait to see."

"But if you should...should go early, what are your wishes?"

"Let's think positively. If it's a boy I hope you'd name him Clarence with a double name. My father's name was Charles Sean and grandfather's name was Jesse Daniel. Do those names appeal to you?"

"You decide, Claudine."

"Very well, I'll choose the boy name and you choose the girl name. How about that?"

"Fine. If it's a girl...I want to name her Claudine."

"You wouldn't need to name her after me."

"I want to," April said.

"Well, then, how about April Claudine?" she asked smiling.

"Fine," April said. "If it's a girl, she'll be April Claudine."

"A boy? How about Clarence Sean? Grandfather was very fond of Ireland and that led to our father's name."

"I like it," April said. "Now we only have to wait about six months."

Following a rapid light knock on the door, a nurse entered with some medication. "These should make you more comfortable," the nurse said.

"Actually, I'm not hurting," Claudine said.

"Good. I'm in time. These should keep the pain at bay," the nurse said. She handed Claudine the tiny cup of pills and poured a glass of water for her.

April, in the meantime, walked across the room to the window. She thought of the reality of her pregnancy and was, as always, overwhelmed with guilt. Should she tell Claudine the truth? What would happen if she did? She'd surely lose the money.

She bit her lip. *It would serve me right if I did. I don't deserve it. But would I lose it? Maybe Claudine would adopt the baby. Should I tell? Should I? No. Not now. Not while she's mending. It surely would upset her. Later...maybe.*

The nurse left and closed the door behind her.

"I want to ask you how you feel about the antique business," Claudine said. "It was something grandfather started after he began traveling to Europe and became fascinated with history."

"I'll do whatever you want," April said.

"I don't know, dear, but you may not find antiques interesting. We got caught up in it with grandfather's love of it. He used to run his fingers over the handmade carvings and talk about how beauty as well as practicality was important in the old days, in the old countries. He wondered about the men who did the work and sometimes was able to learn something of them and their families. On occasion, he would also find items left intentionally, or by accident, in some of the furniture."

"What did he find?"

"Money sometimes, and letters or notes that were very revealing of love or loss. A few times he found jewelry...a beautiful diamond ring once, although it was of the old mine cut. But these findings were not what appealed to him most. It was the woodwork, the artisanship and the men who created each item. Now, in America, we have a different kind of beauty in the work of the Shakers. You may remember the simple, beautiful lines of the chair I showed you one day in the store."

"Yes, I remember," April said.

"You know we have a reputation. People from New York to California buy from us."

"I know. I've seen some of them," April said.

"Well, what do you think? Would learning the business and carrying on there be of interest to you, or would you rather do something else? Regardless of money, I do strongly believe in work. Everyone needs something to do. Hopefully, something of interest to them. We see the way problems develop in idle people."

"I feel a little scared, Claudine. I need to know so much."

"I'm going to teach you, if you really want to know. Do you have a special interest otherwise? What about when you were in high school? What did you like?"

"I liked most all of my subjects and I was a good student. My special interest was art. I wanted to paint pictures. I asked for an easel for Christmas. There's a carpenter in Watsonville, Mr. Shacklin, who does woodcarving and makes birdhouses. I thought he could make me an easel, but Daddy said art was foolishness. He said what I needed to do was find me some hard working old boy with a decent job and get married up."

"I suppose you didn't get the easel," Claudine said.

"No. Mama said Daddy was the boss and we had to do whatever he said."

"Well, belatedly, you'll get your easel and art lessons if you wish," Claudine said.

"I would love it, Claudine. You're so good to me!"

"Actually, April, art would fit very well in the antique store. You could draw in some original paintings to add to the antique ones we already have."

"You must get well, Claudine. What will I do without you?"

"We'll start lessons in the store as soon as I can get out of this hospital. But you better go now. It's tiring sitting a hospital room a long time."

"I don't mind," April said.

"Well, nevertheless you should go now, and do be careful. Come give me a hug," Claudine said.

After April hugged and kissed Claudine, she left and walked down the hospital corridor thinking again about whether or not she should tell Claudine the truth about the baby. She knew many people would feel that the amazing amount of money was to be kept at all costs. The money, however, dimmed in importance to her when weighed against a lifetime of guilt. She would tell Claudine when the time seemed right and let whatever happened, happen.

Chapter Six

Police Chief Hillman listened as his detective reported on his latest interview, this time with Dell Stembridge.

"I found him with wounds to his head and hand which made him look suspicious," Detective Kelly said.

"How did he explain them?"

"He claimed he was scratched while cleaning brush from around the old Stembridge home place. I saw that brush was piled on the curb, and the surrounding area did appear recently cleared. Still, he could have done that *after* the shooting to have an excuse."

"What was your impression of him?" Hillman asked.

"That he's immature, spoiled, and angry."

"Not a good combination."

"No. He feels he has been cheated. Claims his grandfather favored his cousins and left him out. I asked what his grandfather had done for him," Kelly said. "He admitted he'd been left the old home place and its furnishings, plus a hundred thousand dollars. He claims he also has a hand written note from his grandfather telling him to let him know if he needed more money, but that was years ago when he first entered college. It seems the old man doted on him, even helped spoil him, and probably did mean to leave him more money until he saw him squander it."

"In any event, that doesn't sound much like being left out."

"No, but he claims the antique business his grandfather loved so much is worth far more than he was given. He thinks he should have a partnership interest in it."

"A hundred thousand almost spent. How?"

"College and living expenses he claims. He dropped out of college after a semester, though. And get this...he thinks there may be money in Swiss banks while his money has virtually evaporated. Truth of the matter is, he spent the money at gambling houses."

"So he's looking for more money."

"Exactly, but Miss Stembridge doesn't think she owes him anything.

She points out, in regard to the inheritance, that there were two of them, she and Clarence, while Dell was only one. She claims before their grandfather died he saw Dell as a wastrel. He's been a thorn in her side because he keeps pressuring her," Kelly said.

"Do you think he shot her?"

"I don't know, but I think he bears watching. Miss Stembridge thinks his gambling has put him deep in debt. I think he could go to most any length to make the claim. He spoke of seeking an attorney, but I doubt it will do him any good."

"So that leaves him desperate," the Chief said.

"Yes, but he does have the old Stembridge mansion that he could sell. It's in need of repair, but it still would bring probably as much as four hundred thousand considering there's also timber on the land."

"Not bad, although he could fritter it away pretty quickly if he kept up his gambling luck," the chief said.

"He might believe the death of his cousins would benefit him, assuming, of course he wasn't found guilty of the deed, but there's still April and the baby. If they were gone, too, he might try to stake a claim as the only remaining Stembridge although I don't know about the legalities there," the chief said with fingertips pressed together. "Do you still think April Stembridge had something to do with her husband's death? If not, she could be in danger, too."

"I'm not sure. I'm checking on her boyfriend. Some pictures I have reveal Lewisburg, West Virginia, as his home.

He probably didn't realize anyone would check, but the name of the town became visible on a store. That is, it did under magnification. I'll see what I can find out about him in his hometown."

***

Matton Lennet called to his son, Dawson, to join him, then he quickly locked the front door of his antique store.

"We'll offer our services to Miss Stembridge if she's available, but if not, we'll offer to help April. I want you to take special notice of April, Daw. You're about the same age, and she's available now," Matton said.

Daw made no comment. The tall, young man bore the dark coloring of his Hawaiian mother. He was not particularly good looking having inherited his father's coarse facial features, but he had a pleasant voice. People were always asking him if he sang, but he'd never really tried. Basketball had been his love.

"It would be a real plus for us...for you, Daw, if we could bring our two stores together," Matton said.

"We have too much junk, Dad. I don't think she would want me or the junk."

"Not junk, really, Daw, just less valuable items in some cases. That's good, though. It gives the customer a range of choices. And don't put yourself down."

"I don't think the Stembridges would go for it," Daw said.

"Don't be too sure. If you and April were to hit it off, it could change Miss Claudine's way of thinking."

"Dad, I've got a girl friend. I don't think Frances would like to share me."

Matton sighed. "Boy, think beyond that girl. What does Frances have to offer? Nothing except good looks, and April has that and wealth."

"You go for her. She likes old men," Daw said.

"Stop that! Besides I'm not looking to marry again," Matton said.

"I guess marriage didn't suit you too well," Daw said, "since you left Mama in Hawaii."

"Well, I raised you pretty well myself, didn't I? Nealeana wouldn't have fit in living in Columbus, Mississippi. You know that. I told you."

"All I know is I was seven years old and wanted to be with her," Daw said. "I'm going to see her somehow as soon as I can raise the money."

"Daw, she married again and has got other kids, but if you really mean to go, win April and you'll have plenty of money for the trip."

"You get your handyman to marry her. Duggar's sneaky and mean. He'll do anything for a few bucks," Daw said.

"Son, you know better than that. You're pretty mean yourself to shoot off your mouth to me. I've done the best by you I could."

"Like keeping me working so I messed up my schooling and missed out on basketball?"

"What's basketball? A short time thing. You have a whole business coming to you. It was best you learned about it."

"Junk," Daw said.

"Much more than junk if you win April Stembridge. Time may come when she has that business all to herself. Might even be sooner than some think."

"I told you I'm not interested, and she wouldn't be interested in me. She's used to fine living."

"She's not long used to it. I know old Vel Johnson and his mud-ugly wife. They ain't nothing, and if you come from nothing, you ain't nothing."

"Like I said, I'm going to Hawaii to see my mother."

"How? You ain't got traveling money."

"I would have if you paid me better."

I'm not for you wasting our money. Besides, the business is gonna be yours one of these days."

Daw stopped in his tracks. " 'One of these days.' More like one of these *years*. Now you come up with this April thing. No, Pop. No! I'm out of here!" He took a few steps away and then began to run hard. "Yahooooo!" he shouted throwing his arms in the air.

"Get yourself back here, you crazy boy," Matton yelled, but Daw was already out of earshot.

***

Sitting at his desk in the police station John Kelly made telephone calls to West Virginia. The police department in Lewisburg had no record of Mitchell Redmond, but Kelly was referred to nearby Beckley where some Redmonds were listed. So, Kelly reasoned, the fine home in Lewisburg apparently belonged to someone else.

Kelly immediately called the police department at Beckley. The detective who responded said, "Yes, we know the Redmond families. Coal miners in the past, but more recently most of them work in construction jobs. Mitchell? We were in high school together. He was a good student, very bright and ambitious, but his family was too poor to send him to college. I suppose that's why he joined the air force and learned to fly planes."

"Do you know if he's married?" Kelly asked.

"Yeah. Got a pretty wife and a couple of little kids. His wife, Marlene, stays here near her parents. Her parents aren't well. I understand Mitch comes home when he can on leave."

"No negatives about him?" Kelly asked.

"No. None that I know of."

Kelly replaced the telephone and rubbed his eyes. No negatives? Well, two at least. He was a liar and a cheat. Did he plan to divorce his wife and marry April? That would certainly allow him to have a mansion like the one he claimed in the photograph.

Kelly picked up the telephone again and dialed April's number.

"Hello," he said, when she answered the phone. "I wasn't sure you'd be there. Is Miss Claudine home from the hospital?"

"No. I'm going over to be with her in about an hour."

"Fine. I want to see you for a few minutes," Kelly said.

"Very well, if you come right on," April said.

"Is ten minutes soon enough?"

"Oh, you always tease. Just come on," April said.

In ten minutes, she saw him pull into the driveway. He seemed to hurry getting out of his car. What was so urgent? Did he have some news about the killer?

This time she remembered security and dealt with it. No comment from him but he grinned and raised his eyebrows. He was not serious. Oh, then probably no important news.

"What do you want to see me about this time?" she asked.

"Maybe we better go sit in our usual places in the parlor," he said.

"Oh?" *Maybe this is serious.*

When they were seated he said, "You may remember I asked you if your boyfriend was married."

"Former boyfriend," she emphasized. "Yes, I remember but I don't think so."

"If he claimed he's single, he lied. He's not only married, but father of two children."

"Oh!" April cried, "Oh, no!" She paled and fought off tears.

"I see that hurt," he said, "you must still care."

"No. It's...it's just I'm shocked. I'd never have dated him if I knew he was married."

"All right, and the pictures...false, too. He's from a poor family. So he may have plans for your money."

"No, that's not true."

"How do you know?"

"Okay, I guess I'll tell you. I wanted to marry him, but he turned me down."

"But aren't you pregnant with his baby?"

"Who told you that? No! I hate you for even suggesting it!"

"It's not original with me," Kelly said.

"You can forget that. I admit I was in love with him at one time, but that changed."

"When he wouldn't marry you? When did you propose? Before or after your husband's murder."

"I told you I dated him *before* I married Clarence. Why can't you get that straight?"

"Well, for one thing I know you telephoned him twice in the days before your husband's murder. Was that when you proposed?"

"You know, Detective, you can really be rude. The times I telephoned him had to do with whether or not I'd lost my earrings in his car. Not on that day of course. Earlier when we had dated. Later, I found them and called to tell him not to bother with hunting them. That's two phone calls. Right?"

"Yes, but I wonder about the content since you were so in love you wanted to marry him."

"I told you I changed my mind when he was hateful. I don't want to ever see him again."

"You didn't tell me he was hateful."

"At one point he was."

"So you turned him off like turning off a water faucet when he refused your proposal."

"No, I tried to hold on and I bawled like a fool, but I...well, I don't want a marriage like...like somebody I know."

"I didn't expect you to be so candid. He must have really hurt you."

"He did, but I'm through with him."

"Interesting. How're you feeling? I mean with being pregnant?"

"I'm good. Is that all? I need to check on Claudine."

"Yes, that's all for now."

They walked to the front door in silence. He went out and she set the security system on.

***

Kelly was not satisfied. He still had a feeling that Redmond could somehow be involved and would show up again on April's doorstep after a divorce...for the wealth. But why did he have to be hateful to her? He guessed Redmond didn't want to be bothered by a clinging woman and was vain enough to think he could get her back whenever he wanted. She even admitted she tried to hang on. Still, if she really meant to stand her ground, he might find winning her again more difficult than he would expect.

Kelly decided to investigate further. He drove to Hector's nightclub. Maybe an interview with Aero would give a clue to the puzzle.

As before, in the daytime, there were no vehicles around except the one old van. Kelly parked his car and hesitated as someone was opening the front door of the nightclub...a skinny woman. The detective left his car and approached the stranger.

"Excuse me, do you work here?" Kelly asked.

"No. My boyfriend does."

"Your boyfriend? Would that be Hector?"

"No. The bouncer. Aero. Why?"

"Aero is the one I'd like to talk with. I'm Detective John Kelly."

"A detective? Is Aero in trouble?"

"Routine questioning. Where can I locate him?"

"I don't think you can, Detective. He's on a locked ward at the hospital. Gone crazy."

"How so?"

"Nightmares and thinking things that ain't so. Like thinking a captain is his dead brother...stuff like that. It got him in trouble...in a fight with a jealous husband. Aero told me the wife was too friendly with the captain. Anyway, Aero damn near killed that poor husband. You know Aero was a boxer, so he's real strong."

"I would think so."

"They put the man in the hospital and Aero in jail. Then they saw Aero was crazy so they hauled him off to the looney ward."

"And who are you, Miss?"

"I'm Helen Madison. I'd help Aero, but I don't know how. He's just gone off the deep end."

"Was he using drugs or alcohol?"

She hesitated. "Alcohol, and that made him guilty. He'd sworn off booze, but he couldn't resist it," she said.

"Which hospital is he in?" Kelly asked.

"That one out on the highway going toward Alabama. It's called Hill Psychiatric Hospital."

"Thanks," Kelly said. He got back into his car thinking. *'Alcohol.' Probably, drugs, too and plenty of them. But what does that have to do with the Stembridge problem? Maybe nothing.* He felt frustrated and banged his forehead with the heel his hand.

He headed back to the police station. He wanted to talk with the chief and see if any other information had come in by way of the deputies.

In the chief's office, Kelly said, "The only suspect I haven't interviewed is Matton Lennet. Somehow I doubt his wanting to buy Stembridge Antiques makes him a murderer, but I'm about at my wits end."

"Some detail we haven't uncovered yet is *the key*," Chief Hillman said. "Some hidden fact, but what? You're doing all you can Kelly, but I hate to see the time slipping by." He sat up straight and tapped his pencil on a pad as he often did. "Some detail, some hidden fact we have yet to uncover. Well, go ahead and interview Lennet, but I agree with you that he's probably not who we're looking for."

***

April brought a cheerful Claudine home from the hospital. Although her complexion had taken on a slight yellowish cast, it was hard to think of her as terminally ill when she seemed so upbeat. Still, it was clear she was fighting weakness as she held on to her cane to walk.

"Tell you what, April," Claudine said. "Let's go shopping tomorrow."

"Shopping? Are you sure you feel up to it?"

"Definitely. I want to help choose things for the baby. And, by the way, we must decide how to decorate the room adjacent to yours. That can be the nursery, don't you think?"

"Yes. Perfect," April said.

"We'll look at wallpaper and shop for the baby's furniture. This is going to be such a thrill," Claudine said clasping her hands together. "Oh, now don't worry. I know we can't do it all in one day, but we need to get started. You're about four months along now, aren't you?"

"Yes," April said, "and doing well now that the morning sickness has passed."

"What colors should we choose...not all yellow although yellow is a cheerful color, especially the soft shades. Probably we should select both some blue and some pink...oh, I don't know. We'll see what we can find."

April smiled. "We'll have a good time choosing," she said. *No way can I tell Claudine the truth about the baby now that she's so happy.*

"In a way," Claudine said, "I wish we knew whether the baby is a boy or a girl, oh, but I know what we can do! We'll buy two complete outfits; one in blue and one in pink along with some yellow. Then we'll donate the color that doesn't match to the child welfare office for some little ones who can use it. Yes, that way we don't really have to know for sure."

"Great," April said. "You can let me know what day you feel like shopping."

"Fine. I hope it will be tomorrow, but I'll let you know," Claudine said.

***

Marvelous Johnson was not happy. He paced the front porch of his house, thinking. Here he had a rich daughter, and she held off giving him money. She should be building him a great house and buying him anything he wanted. Everybody said the Stembridges had millions, and yet his widowed young'un had not given him ten cents. She was a mama's girl. Of course! Why hadn't he thought of that before? He'd get Flaudie Mae to work a deal. Too bad that old Claudine gal survived the shooting. He'd hoped she'd croak and then there'd be no question of a joint bank account.

He left the porch and went inside to open a desk drawer. He removed the notebook he wrote his farm supplies in, pulled a chair up and sat down.

Flaudie Mae walked in. "What are you doing?" she asked.

"I'm fixin' to make a list of what you're going to tell April we need," he said.

"Oh, Vel, don't do that. She's not in full charge of her account yet."

"Well, she's gonna be. I aim to see to it, so it's not too early to let her know what you want from her."

"Me? I'm not asking for anything."

"Yes, you are. She'll give plenty to you as soon as she can. You're gonna need a heap of things, a big, new Dodge Ram truck for starters."

"You're going to make things hard for her, Vel. Don't you care about her?"

"Don't she care about me is the thing here. Ain't I her daddy what raised her?"

"Well, yes, but we need to think of her."

"No, buts about it. This is gonna happen and soon. I'm makin' the list now." He picked up a pencil, stuck the writing end in his mouth, then took the wet lead out and started writing.

***

Next morning April waited for Claudine to come to breakfast. When she did not show up by nine o'clock, April knocked on her bedroom door. Still no answer. April opened the door gently and called to her. Still no answer. April's heart raced as she walked to the bed and lifted back the cover near Claudine's face. She gasped and then she screamed.

Mary Jean came running. April grabbed hold of the girl in an embrace and sobbed. "She's dead! She's dead."

Mary Jean held April close although she was trembling herself.

"She seemed so well yesterday," April cried. " So well, and we were going shopping today for the baby."

"Yes, ma'am." Mary Jean said. "They says when somebody real sick is feeling too good one day, they don't last."

"But the very next day!" April cried.

"I know. That's the way it be sometimes. We sure gonna miss her. She was such a good lady."

April stood back and looked at Mary Jean. "She was so looking forward to the baby. Oh, I'm so sad for her and I don't know what I'm going to do. She was going to help me learn the business."

Chapter Seven

Once again the Stembridge mansion was filled with police, although on the surface it did not appear Claudine had been murdered. The preliminary medical examinations were made befo re her body was removed for an autopsy.

April wept and trembled with the realization that she was now faced with all decisions concerning the Stembridge business and possessions. She in no way felt ready for it and she could think of no one who could help her. She would have to do it alone with the help of the attorney whom she'd never met. That was to have happened soon. Claudine had planned to arrange the meeting once she returned home from the hospital. Oh, what was his name? She had heard it but she couldn't remember. Surely he would show up and identify himself. First of all there was the funeral to plan as soon as the autopsy was complete. Jayson helped Claudine to plan Clarence's funeral. Maybe he could help with Claudine's, too.

John Kelly came across the room and took her hand. "I'm sorry," he said. *At least he doesn't think I killed Claudine.*

In the confusion and pain, April had forgotten to call her parents. She went upstairs to her bedroom and dialed their number. Her mother answered.

"Claudine is dead," April cried.

"Dead?" her mother asked.

"Yes. You know she had terminal cancer, but I didn't expect it to take her so soon."

"We'll come right on as soon as your daddy gets in from feeding the dogs."

***

Hunter Warren left his law office on Main Street and exited the stone building. He had known the Stembridge family for forty years. Clarence and Claudine were children when their grandfather became his client. Today the distinguished grayhaired lawyer felt saddened by the death of Claudine and troubled by Clarence's unsolved murder. He'd liked Claudine Stembridge and admired her devotion to Clarence after his accident. Now there was the young woman who would inherit the Stembridge fortune. He hoped she was a deserving person who would use her inheritance in a way the Stembridge family would prefer. It seemed unfair that Claudine and Clarence would never be able to see the child who would continue their family into another generation. But who ever said that life was fair? Today he would go to the home for a brief visit, then have April come to his office later to deal with the wills.

After a short drive, Lawyer Warren reached the Stembridge mansion. As he had expected, the home was swarming with officials and visitors inside. He saw Detective Kelly and spoke to him. "Could we confer a moment in private?" Warren asked.

"Certainly," Kelly said. "Let's walk down to the library. I don't think it's occupied at the moment."

When they were alone, the attorney asked, "Are you close to making an arrest, John?"

"I wish I could say so, but not yet. We're following all leads, but have nothing solid. No clear suspects, yet. As you know, police work can be frustrating and tedious at times."

"Yes, I know," Warren said. "Remember I was on the force at one point."

"I know."

"What about the young Mrs. Stembridge? Do you know anything that would lead you to suspect she had a hand in the deaths?"

"I felt suspicious of her at first for obvious reasons. Now, however, I doubt she had anything to do with Mr. Stembridge's murder, and I'm convinced she is truly devastated by Miss Claudine's death."

"Then you believe she is innocent in all respects?" Warren asked.

"I do. However, at this point, everyone is open to investigation."

"I'll be most interested in knowing who is responsible," Warren said.

"So will we," Kelly said.

"Do tell me anything you think I should know. April is to inherit a great deal of money and I'd like to believe she's worthy of the trust my late clients put in her," Warren said.

Kelly chose not to mention speculation about the paternity of April's baby. The suspicion could be false. In an epiphany, he realized he didn't want to believe the accusation himself! Well, DNA could settle the matter if necessary. Dell, in an effort to disqualify April, would most likely raise the question.

"You seem to be hesitating," Warren said.

"Just thinking," Kelly said. "We'll deal with any realities that come up, but for now, I'm afraid we have nothing to justify an arrest."

***

Kelly believed questioning Matton Lennet a waste of time, but he set out to interview the man since Lennet was on Miss Claudine's list of possible suspects. He had seen the scruffy-looking little man around town, almost always with a stubby cigar rolling from one side of his mouth to the other. Lennet looked out with watchful eyes from beneath bushy eyebrows, head thrust forward, as if he expected to see something unusual. Kelly thought it must be Lennet's habit in constantly searching for a find for his antique store, but who knew why?

Kelly parked in front of Lennet's Antiques. The store lacked the classy appearance of Stembridge's. Still, it had a certain appeal as an unpainted, pioneer style home. An old wagon and other antiques cluttered the front yard.

Dugger stood on a long truck bed, shirtless, revealing his hairy back and arms. His muscles rippled as he unloaded a heavy dresser. Kelly had seen Dugger wrestle and walk away the winner every time. He wondered when other young men would give up, but most every Saturday night a new opponent would show up. Kelly thought Dugger with his bearded face and small, dark eyes looked the part of fierce strength, but he'd heard him speak softly in his uneducated manner.

"Good morning," Kelly said.

" 'Mornin' Captain," Dugger said.

"Is Mr. Lennet in?"

"Yes, Sir. Jest go right on through that there door," Dugger said pointing to the office door. A wider sliding door at the end of the building was open to receive the furniture Dugger was unloading, but he would need to carry it across a porch. Wonder why he didn't use a cart of some kind with wheels? However, he seemed to have no trouble managing the heavy load.

Kelly opened the office door and found Lennet wiping tears and started to excuse himself.

"No, come on in," Lennet said. He sniffed and laid his dirty handkerchief on his desk still clutching it in his fist.

"Are you sick?" Kelly asked.

"Naw, it's my boy. Daw left me and went to Hawaii. He's all I got, and I've lived my whole life, since the day he was born, thinking of him."

"Perhaps he'll return," Kelly said.

"I don't think so, but his being gone is like taking away my reason for living. I always thought of what would be best for him. He didn't understand that. I don't know why. It was like I almost lived in his skin the same as mine." Lennet spoke looking down at his hand, slowly squeezing his wadded handkerchief. "Not a day passed but what I didn't set him down and say, 'tell me about your day, son.' He told me when he was

little, but when he got to be about thirteen I'd have to pick it out of him. I loved hearing everything my boy did. Bought him protection when he told me about having sex. He told me every detail and I just lived like in his skin same as mine."
"Didn't he want some privacy?" Kelly asked.
"Yeah, sometimes he'd get up to leave, but I'd call him back. Seems like he couldn't understand how I loved hearing everything in his life. He was a big boy, tall, you know, six foot three and wanted to play basketball, but I thought that was wasting time. He didn't like me holding back on money either, but I was saving for him." Lennet looked up and said, "I saved enough, too, I was gonna have a good down payment on the Stembridge store if the Stembridges reached a point to sell. Now Daw knew that, but he couldn't get over wanting to go to Hawaii to see Nealeana."
"Nealeana?"
"His mother."
"I'm sorry about your troubles, but I'm making routine investigations, Mr. Lennet. I need to know where you were the night Mr. Stembridge was murdered?"
"What?"
"Where were you the night Clarence Stembridge was murdered?"
"I wasn't nowhere. I mean I didn't go no place. Went to bed early and didn't know anything about him until the next morning."
"Who could verify that?"
"Daw, but he ain't here. Like I said he's gone to Hawaii."
"How about Dugger?"
"He wasn't around. He lives in that shack down by the creek bridge."
Kelly hesitated. "I see."

"I didn't kill him," Lennet said. "Can't think why you'd even ask."

"Where were you when Miss Claudine was shot?"

"Now you're about to make me mad. I can tell you that, though. I was right here in my store with a customer. A lady named Mary Smith was here fingering a chest I bought that morning. Yes, and she bought it. You can ask her."

"I don't know the lady. What's her address?"

"I gave the paper to Dugger and he lost it. Probably, though, she's in the phone book," he said but he didn't reach for a telephone book.

"Let's look it up," Kelly said.

"Aw, I don't know where that dang phone book is. Maybe you can find it at your place, Detective."

"How can you run a business if you don't keep records, Mr. Lennet?"

"Oh, I do keep 'em, but don't always write down the customer's name...just the amount of the sale and what it was."

"Where in Hawaii is your son?"

"I don't know the name of the place. Some small town on the big island. I'll let you know if I get a letter from him."

"What's his mother's name?"

"Nealeana."

"Yes, but her last name?"

"Something like Woody or Woodson. Married somebody from Chicago or New York, I think."

"How would you contact her if you needed to?"

"She don't want nothing more to do with me. I don't contact her." Lennet picked a stubby cigar out of the ash tray on his desk and stuck it in his mouth.

"You have no information on how to get in touch with her. Is that what you're saying?"

"Righto!" Lennet said pointing a finger at Kelly, then made a production of lighting his cigar stub.

"I'll be back in touch," Kelly said. He rose to take his leave. What he thought was a useless trip, he now believed may not have been. He would check with Hawaiian authorities immediately to see if the former Nealeana Lennet could be found.

***

Two weeks after Claudine's funeral, April removed the large black ribbon bow from the door to the Antique store. She unlocked the door, switched on the light and went inside. Her vision blurred with tears, but she wiped them away. Although Claudine had given her freedom of choice, she wanted to honor the Stembridge family by continuing their work if possible. It still had not sunk in how wealthy she was, but the honor and trust had touched her deeply and made her feel determined to do what she could to honor the family name.

She found company ledgers in the office and began to look through them. One book showed the current stock and was heavily labeled...a blessing complete with pictures, cost of the item and selling price. Then there were notes penned in Claudine's small script. April sighed. Maybe she could do this after all. At least with the current stock, although she knew she would have much to learn when it came to making purchases.

She ran her hand over the increased mound of her stomach. What about when the baby came? She knew she would need help in the store. Maybe she should run an ad in the *Commercial Dispatch*. Yes, she'd do that. She sat at the desk and wrote up the requirements for the job as best she could. How much should she pay? She'd have to feel her way on that one. An experienced sales person would say what he or she had been paid. Yes, checking references would shed some light. No use to wait. She'd take the ad by the newspaper office immediately and hope a qualified person would apply.

Before she left, she listened to recorded messages on the telephone. There were several orders and inquires from out of state. She listened carefully and made notes, replaying the messages several times. Could she do this? She took her list through the store looking for requested items and found three she thought could be of interest to the callers. She returned to the office and made each of the calls. To her great surprise and pleasure, all three were sales! Now to call the shipping company and get the orders packed and shipped.

Little more than an hour later, she locked the door feeling lighthearted. So far, so good! She'd drop by the *Commercial Dispatch*, leave the ad then go back home, but tomorrow she'd be back in the store by nine o'clock.

***

Kelly drove out of Columbus on Highway 45 to Hill Psychiatric Hospital. He thought perhaps after three weeks Aero would be in better condition and maybe able to be interviewed.

At the front desk, the chubby receptionist stopped typing on the computer and looked at Kelly over her plastic, rose-rimmed glasses. "May I help you?" she asked.

"I'd like to see Mr. Aero Laston."

"He was discharged this morning, Sir."

"Thanks." Kelly fingered the little wooden sign on her desk that read, "Everybody does not hate you. Everybody does not know you."

"Where'd you get your sign?" he asked.

"I don't know. Somebody left it here." She turned back to the computer and began typing.

Kelly shrugged and walked out the front door. He checked his watch. Four seventeen. He'd drive on out to Hector's and see what he could learn.

***

Hector was alone when Kelly arrived. "Well, well, Detective I see you're paying us another visit. You're welcome, but I doubt we'll be any help."

"Is Aero around now?"

"No. He's with his girlfriend, Helen. I think you met her."

"I did. She told me about his mental problem."

"Yeah, he really went bonkers. Actually, I don't think he's straight yet. Straight, ha! Won't never be."

"What do you mean?"

"He's a switch hitter."

"Bisexual?"

"Yeah."

"How does his girl friend feel about that?" Kelly asked.

"She seems not to know. Like that night he beat up that guy who had to be hospitalized...he wasn't a jealous husband. He was a gay attempting to charm the captain."

"Michael Redmond?"

"Yeah, that's him."

"Do you think Redmond is bisexual?"

"Don't know, but a lot of pretty guys are," Hector said.

"Have you seen anything that made you think he might be?"

"No. He's always surrounded by women, but once in a while a gay makes an effort to get his attention."

"How does Redmond react to that?"

"Friendly, but he's friendly to everybody. I haven't seen anything that made me think he's interested in the guys. I think he's just a vain fellow who loves having all the attention he can get."

"Do you know where Aero and Redmond were the night Mr. Stembridge was murdered?"

"No. Neither one of them was here. Aero asked off so he could take Helen out to celebrate her birthday. Redmond? Just don't know," Hector said. "Do you suspect them in some way?" "Still in the process of checking everything," Kelly said. "I hope you catch the murderer and the one who tried to kill Miss Claudine. I didn't know the Stembridges, but heard they were really nice folks."

Kelly left thinking his next question would be put to Helen. She could tell him when and where they celebrated her birthday...if that happened. Still, what possible motive would Aero have to harm the Stembridges? He might check with April on Dell Stembridge again. He was a more likely suspect.

***

Kelly found April at the store, talking with some delicate-appearing young man and waited just inside the door. It appeared the interview was over as April gathered up some papers and stood. "I'll let you know," she said.

The very blond young man stood and bowed slightly. "I do hope I'll be chosen. I don't think you'd be disappointed in my work."

"Thank you for coming in. I'll let you know," April said.

The slender young man walked past Kelly and nodded before he opened the door and left.

"Are you planning to employ help?" Kelly ask.

"Yes, and that young man seems to be well qualified. He grew up working in antiques with his mother. He also studied architecture and related subjects at Mississippi State."

"Are you planning, then, to employ him?"

"I'm not sure. I'll check his references. He appears to be a little on the feminine side. Do you think that would be a problem with customers?" April asked.

"You're asking my opinion?"

"Yes, that was a question. There was a little question mark at the end of the sentence."

Kelly laughed. "You're pretty sassy, aren't you?"

"Ah, a question. I recognize it. Yes, sometimes."

"I don't know. Some people might prefer a more masculine clerk, but I think most people wouldn't care if he served them well."

"Thanks. I really did want your opinion." She smiled. "Claudine told me the importance of being careful about employing people. I'm trying to make judgments when I talk with them, but that's not enough. Claudine said once she employed a charming woman without first checking references. Guess what? She said the woman turned out to be a liar and a thief. So I'm going to be a reference checker."

"A good idea," Kelly said.

"Let's sit at this table over by the front window. I have another person coming in for an interview."

When they were seated, April continued. "Another thing, Claudine said people get passed over sometimes because of how they look. I was wondering about that just now, you know. I thought about Mary Jean with her being an albino. But Claudine saw Mary Jean was both good and smart. And Jayson was a farm boy, not an experienced chauffer, but he knew a lot about machines, was strong and a good person." April sighed deeply. "So much to consider and I lack her wisdom. Oh, I miss her so much!"

"I can see why, but you seem to be thinking things through," Kelly said.

"I'm trying. Do you have any news?" April asked.

"No. Nothing definite. I thought I'd ask you if you have any."

"I don't. I wish I did," she said.

"What about Dell? Has he been bothering you again?"

"He's asking for money. I told him I understood he'd already received his inheritance and gambled it away."

"What did he say?"

"That he received less than his fair share because somebody complained to his grandfather that he was irresponsible. I said, 'well, you were and you are.' He said, 'April, people can change. I've learned my lesson.' I said, 'Dell, if you're not found guilty, I'll make you a one-time gift of some money.' "

"Do you really mean to give him money? What was his reaction to that?"

"He smiled and declared his innocence. He wanted money immediately, but I said, 'not a dime until this case is solved and you are proven innocent.' He begged but I stood firm. I also said before I'd give him money I wanted him to write down his debts and be honest about it. I wanted him to promise in writing that he'd never gamble again, sign and date it."

"He agreed to that?"

"He did. I reminded him this would be a one-time gift so he'd better grow up and handle it in a responsible way."

"You're generous to even consider it. Does your lawyer agree with this? I'd think Hunter Warren might advise against it," Kelly said.

"Mr. Warren has been very kind, but I didn't ask him. I don't really care much for Dell, but I realize people make mistakes and maybe he needs a second chance. I mean to give him that chance...if, as I said, he's not the murderer."

"Has anyone else been leaning on you for money?"

"Nobody else but my dad. He started just after I was married and has never let up. I'm sorry to say this, but my dad is a rather spoiled person who expects a lot from other people. At that time I told him I was on a joint account with Claudine and would need her approval. Well, he immediately wanted me to get a lawyer to get my funds separate so I could give him money. Of course, I refused that."

"Now what?"

"I'm going to build him and Mama a nice house in Watsonville and, yes, I'll give him a sizeable amount of money. Like with Dell, however, I intend to tell him he'll need to manage on the gift rather than keep coming back for more."

"He would keep coming back?"

She laughed. "You better believe it. His wants are endless."

"I'm impressed with your maturity. Are you sure you're only nineteen?"

"I'm sure I'm not. I had a birthday. I'm twenty now."

"How're you feeling?"

"I'm good except I'd be better if Claudine were here." Tears blurred her vision, but she wiped them away with the back of her hand.

"I'm sorry," he said. He stood. "I'll be going now. Take care of yourself. I hope you make a good choice on your employee."

"Thanks," she said. "Bye."

Chapter Eight

Kelly hated to go to the chief's with nothing concrete to report, but he knew he was expected to check in from time to time. This was the time, or maybe somewhat past it. He had stalled long enough, he thought, as he approached the door. He found the chief on the telephone and slipped quietly in a chair across from the desk.

"All right. I'll pick it up on the way home," Chief Hillman said before he hung up the phone and turned to Kelly.

"Any news?"

"Sorry, still nothing solid. It appears any of the suspects could be guilty. I don't remember a case where a good man had so many people who could have killed him."

"Has it occurred to you that the Stembridge's troubles began after April came into their lives?" Chief Hillman said.

Kelly frowned. "I hadn't thought of it exactly that way. Hummm, I wonder. Well, I have from the beginning suspected the captain she was dating. Now a thought crosses my mind. Another possible suspect could be her father from what I hear of him."

"Her father?"

"Yes. He started demanding money right after she married Clarence. According to April, he's never let up. I'm sure she didn't mean to suggest he's a murderer, but she describes him as a spoiled person who expects others to cater to him. But would he murder for money?"

"I'd say that's a possibility if he's money hungry in a big way. Have you met him?"

"No, but I'll look him up and check him out," Kelly said. "What's his name?"

"Marvelous Johnson."

"Oh, I've heard of him," Chief Hillman said. "He was jailed once here in Columbus for breaking and entering a business. A grocery store, if I remember correctly. Yes, definitely, check him out."

"I'll put him next on the list," Kelly said.

"Good. Let me know what you find."

"Yes, Sir, I will." Kelly rose and left the chief's office to go to his own. He wanted to make a couple of telephone calls first ... one to Hawaii and one to Helen Madison.

Helen apparently was not at home, and the police detective in Hawaii said he'd call back when he could check the matter out.

***

Kelly drove the thirty-one miles to Watsonville and stopped at a gas station to ask directions to Marvelous Johnson's home. The young boy who gassed up his car gave directions. "Yes, Sir," the teenager said, "Mr. Vel lives right on down this road 'bout three miles on the right. It's a kinda little white house with paint wearin' flaky. Old brown checked couch on the porch. You'll recognize it right off."

"Thanks," Kelly said. He paid for the gas bill in cash and drove off down the worn blacktop road. On the way, he noticed a line of pink-blossomed Mimosa trees on the right side of the road. Down almost to the Johnson house, a large pecan orchard stood in deep rows back from the road. He thought nature provided a pleasant scene, unlike the largely unkempt homes and sheds along the three-mile drive. Well, a better section of town might be on other streets, but seeing the housing here, he thought April had done herself a favor by moving to Columbus...even if she hadn't found the Stembridge job. More important, getting away from her father, must feel better. Still, he hadn't met the man. He'd wait and make his own judgment.

The boy's description was perfect. Kelly stopped his car in the driveway close to the side of the house. The old-fashioned country yard was scraped clean of grass and swept. Scraggly shrubs surrounded the porch, and a basket of lavender petunias hung from a hook near the swing.

Kelly mounted the wooden steps to the porch and knocked on the screen door. The aroma of fried country ham and turnip greens made him hungry. He'd not been aware of the noon hour until now.

A thin woman in a clean cotton print dress came to the door. Although her face was unattractive with a broad nose and receding chin she had a kindly expression. "Yes, Sir," she said. "Could I help you?"

"I'm looking for Mr. Marvelous Johnson."

"He's my husband. Not here right now, but should be back any minute. Won't you come in. We're about to have some dinner."

"I'm sorry if I came at an inconvenient time."

"No, it's all right. Have you had your dinner? Oh, I know some folks call it 'lunch', but it's dinner to us country people."

"It really smells good, but I'll go up town and return later...after you've had your meal." He turned to go when an old brown pickup drove behind his car and parked.

She said, "There's Vel now. No use for you to go uptown to one of them fast food things when we got plenty here. Besides, Vel has you blocked."

"Ma'am, I'm a detective. You may not find my company pleasant."

"Oh, your job has nothing to do with it. You're a hungry gentleman so you just come on in and eat with us."

Marvelous slammed the door to his truck and walked as fast as his pudgy body would go to the house and up the steps. "Whose car is that?" he demanded.

"Mr. Johnson, it's mine. I'm Detective Kelly from the Columbus Police Department and I want to ask you a few questions."

"Like what? A detective, you say? What questions?"

"I'll wait until you've had your meal and then we'll talk." She said, "I asked him to eat with us."

"Yeah, hell, come on in. Flaudie Mae ain't no beauty but she can cook like a Miss America."

Kelly glanced at Mrs. Johnson and saw she'd dropped her head. "You're a fortunate man," Kelly said.

"Yeah, well come on. Let's eat."

Kelly shrugged. He felt trapped. With mixed feelings, he walked with the couple into the dining room.

Mrs. Johnson indicated a chair at the round oak table. "You just sit over there and make yourself at home," she said.

"This is a feast," Kelly said. "Everything I like from creamy whipped potatoes, homemade cornbread and country ham."

"So what did you want to ask me?" Marvelous asked.

Kelly said, "Let's wait until after lunch to talk about that. In the meantime, tell me about April. She seems like such a fine young lady."

"Oh, you know April," Mrs. Johnson said. She smiled.

"Yes."

"She's rich now," Marvelous said, "but she ain't give me a dime."

"It's not up to her to support us," Flaudie Mae said.

"I raised her didn't I?" Marvelous said.

"We had a lot of help from my mother," Flaudie Mae said. She glanced at Kelly. "My mother lived next door and she practically raised April, because Vel and I worked most of the time."

"I drove a dump truck six days a week," Marvelous said. "She stayed home."

"I did most of the farming," Flaudie Mae said. "I didn't kill the hogs, but I worked up the meat, including curing this ham." Marvelous slapped Flaudie Mae's arm. "She do make a pretty good old work horse."

Flaudie Mae sighed but said nothing.

"I'd say you're an expert at curing ham, Mrs. Johnson," Kelly said. "This is really the best I've ever eaten."

She smiled. "Thanks."

When the meal was over, Marvelous said, "We'll go out back and sit in a couple of chairs under a shade tree. It'll be cool out there. Besides, I want to show you my dogs."

"Very well," Kelly said.

While they walked out of the house into the back yard, Marvelous said, "Only trouble with having my dogs is, I just suffer terrible when one dies."

Kelly said, "We can get very attached. Dogs make wonderful pets, and some do great work helping handicapped people."

"Yeah, but I think it's wrong to mistreat a dog like that...keeping him all hemmed in with a cripple. Oh, see my prize hounds over there in the pen? I made it really big so they have plenty of romping room."

"Yes, I see they also have a nice house and a swimming pool. You really went all out for them."

"Yeah, I just love them with all my heart," he said, laying his hand on his chest.

"Ah, Mr. Johnson, could we get down to business now? I need to ask you some questions and then I'll be on my way back to Columbus."

"Go ahead. Shoot."

"I have to ask everyone who had any connection to the Stembridge family many of the same questions. So I ask you, where were you on the night of Tuesday, May 2, 2005, the night Mr. Stembridge was murdered?"

"I didn't do that, man! Why you asking me?"

"This is routine questioning. I'm asking many people. Could you just tell me where you were that night?"

"Yeah, I can. Now I didn't set this fight up, and the people who ran it have done moved on, but I went to a cock fight."

"A cock fight? Where?"

"Out by the old cotton gin. A few miles from here," Marvelous said, "you shoulda been there and seen them cocks fight. Blood was everywhere, and they kept going at each other. It was great!"

"You realize that's an illegal activity."

"I know, but I wasn't putting the show on. I just went to enjoy it."

"Are you aware of what's done to those roosters?"

"They're natural fighters so what's the big deal?"

"No, they're not...no more so than other animals. They're tormented to make them aggressive. Drugs such as strychnine and epinephrine are fed to them, and their spurs are cut off and replaced with razor sharp steel blades up to three inches long."

"Yeah, I know, I know, but they ain't nothing but chickens. There was a big crowd there cheering and loving it watching them trapped in their pits to fight it out to the death."

"Who put on this fight?"

"I don't know. Some old boys calling themselves Black and White. I told you they done left for some place out of state. I think they're traveling showmen popping in and out of places for one night stands."

Kelly frowned. "Who did you go with?"

"Nobody. I went by myself."

"Who can verify that?"
"What? You don't believe me?"
"That's not the question. It's a matter of my needing proof."
"Well, I don't reckon you can have it, because nobody I know was there."
Kelly stood. "It was just outside this small town and nobody you know was there? Think hard about that, Mr. Johnson. You may come up with a name of someone that can verify your story."
"Don't think so."
"It might be for your benefit," Kelly said.
"I told you I was by myself, and I sure didn't bump off nobody."
"Yes, Sir, I heard you. Now where were you the morning of June 3, 2005, when Miss Stembridge was shot?"
Marvelous sighed deeply and jabbed his thumb in his belt. "Damn! Well, you can check this one out. I was at Stanley's Farm Equipment looking at a used tractor."
"That's in Columbus?"
"Yeah, and I want you to talk with Stanley hisself. He can tell you I was there."
"Where is that business located?"
"Old Macon Road."
"What address?"
"Oh, I don't know. You can find it if you drive out there...big sign."
Kelly made a note in the little brown notebook he kept in his shirt pocket. "Very well," he said. "By the way, you'll need to move your truck so I can get out."
"Right. I need to run to the store to get some dog food anyway. Gotta feed my babies."

***

Kelly drove into the town of Watsonville to the Police office. The old wooden structure had a sign reading "Watsonville Police Department, Russell Henderson, Chief of Police." Some broken window slats revealed a light on inside. Kelly pushed open the door and walked in.

A boy with shoulder length, brown, curly hair sat behind the desk with an open book in front of him. Kelly judged him to be about fourteen years old.

"Good afternoon." Kelly said. "Is the Chief in?"

"No, sir, he went fishing. I'm his boy, Russell Joe. You can get him on his cell phone if you need him."

"I'll talk with him later. I don't suppose you'd know anything about a cock fight."

"Yes, Sir. I know they was one here a while back."

"Oh, and did you go?"

"No, I don't like that stuff, but some of the men over at the pool hall went. I heard them talking about it."

"Anyone you know?"

"Yes, Sir. Willie Jim Hickson was the main one, but there was others, too. One other was Mr. Johnson."

"Mr. Marvelous Johnson?"

"Yes, Sir, that's him."

"So all of these men went to the fight."

"They talked a lot about it. Mr. Johnson owned a couple of the roosters."

"He owned two of them?"

"Yes, Sir, named them 'Hitler' and 'Saddam Hussein'."

"Well, son, I'm like you. I wouldn't go. That's a cruel thing."

"I like all animals," Russell Joe said, "I aim to be a veterinarian one day."

"Very good. Stick with it."

"You want me to tell Dad you came by?"

"No, I'll call him later." Kelly smiled. "Thanks. Good talking with you," he said.

As he drove back toward Columbus, Kelly considered his trip well worthwhile. He now knew two things about Marvelous Johnson: He was a liar who had broken the law, and he was a self-centered, insensitive man, but it was unlikely he killed Clarence Stembridge. Kelly wondered why the sheriff hadn't arrested him. He knew though, sometimes in small towns, where everybody knew everybody, things could be different. For political or personal reasons, matters were passed over, but he would call Police Chief Russell Henderson and ask some questions.

***

The next morning at ten o'clock, Kelly telephoned the Watsonville Police Department.

"May I speak with Chief Henderson?" Kelly asked.

"You got him," Henderson said.

"Chief, I'm Detective John Kelly, with the Columbus Police Department. I'm questioning a number of people in regard to the Stembridge murder and shooting. You've probably heard of it."

"Yes, sure have. How does that concern me?"

"Nothing directly. In the process of checking out a man in your town, another matter came to my attention and I wanted to mention it to you. A cock fight."

"What do you want to know? As far as I know, Detective, the cock fight is history out here. How does that figure to Columbus?"

"Then you did know of a recent cock fight."

"Yeah, a concerned citizen called and told my wife, but at the time I was down in the bed with the flu. I had my wife call my on-duty policeman, but he wasn't at home. His wife told my wife he'd gone to a chicken show."

"A chicken show?"

"That's what she said, but I knew that meant he was out there at that cock fight." Henderson said. "When he made no arrests, I fired the sucker. Yeah, I knew then he was one of them."

"What about the others involved?"

"Couldn't prove anything on any of them. Hearsay, you know."

"What about Marvelous Johnson?"

"I heard he had some fighting cocks, but when I searched his home place, I couldn't uncover nothing. I found a couple of small dog houses out at the far end of his corn field, like some people keep their chickens in, but he said somebody must have left them there, as they wasn't his."

"Another cock fight may be staged, since you have locals interested in it," Kelly said.

"We'll be on the watch. I got me a new deputy who has a keen eye and ear. Name is Mabel Killins...big, rawboned woman in her thirties who takes no sass and can back it up. Still, she's a good woman. Respected. Plays the organ at the Baptist church."

"Good. I'd appreciate it if you'd let me know if you find anything suspicious is connected to Marvelous Johnson."

"He's a suspect?"

"Everybody is a suspect at this point, Chief. I'm in the process of checking out a lot of people. Since Johnson was connected to that illegal activity, I wanted to talk with you about him. While not directly related to the Stembridge situation, I consider it relates to his character."

"Like I said, I was told about the fight, but just wasn't able to deal with it at the time. Won't happen again with Mabel on the force."

"Let's hope not. Good to talk with you."

"Yeah, call anytime."
Small dog houses? Of course, they were Johnson's, but proof was another matter. Wonder about feathers and other debris in the area, and what about the concerned citizen who telephoned the chief? Kelly thought more effort could have been put into the prosecution of the men involved, but it was not his responsibility. April was fortunate to have been largely brought up by a good grandmother rather than in her parents' home.

Chapter Nine

April found the references satisfying on the thin, blond, somewhat effeminate appearing male applicant. She learned Marvin Reilly had favorably impressed his professors and one former employer in Birmingham, who said she'd employ him again "in a heartbeat."

When she notified Marvin he had the job, she was surprised to learn he was married. He said it was his wife, Lilly, who wanted to move to Columbus from Birmingham. Her parents lived in Aberdeen, a smaller town not far from Columbus.

Marvin said he would need to make shopping trips...with her permission, of course. He named some places in Europe where he had found great items before.

"We'll need to have a proper mark up," Marvin said. "In fact, I suggest we add another ten percent to our selling price. That way if the item doesn't sell in a timely manner, we can reduce the price, put it on sale, and still make a profit."

"Good," April said.

"Do you plan to work in the store, too?" Marvin asked.

"Up to a point," She said, "but I'm thinking you'll need help when I have my baby. Do you have any suggestions?"

"I hope this doesn't sound presumptuous, but Lilly, my wife, would be a big help in the office. She'll be looking for work as a secretary. Then, there's my brother, Eddie, who is just finishing at the University of Alabama. He knows something of the antique business, having been brought up by Mother. I could teach him more...enough so that when I'm away on a buying trip he could keep the store open. He probably wouldn't be a permanent employee, though, as he plans to go to graduate school. Wants to be a psychologist."

"I'd like to meet Lilly and Eddie," April said. "When could they come in?"

"Tomorrow, I think. I'll call you if that's not workable," Marvin said.

***

Through the glass door of the file room, Police Chief Hillman saw Kelly coming down the hall. He hoped for news. Putting aside the file he'd been reviewing, he walked into the hallway.

"Hello, John. I hope you have something to report."

"I do, but not much."

"Let's go in my office and you bring me up to date," Hillman said.

Once they were seated, Kelly told him of his Watsonville experience. "We know Johnson's a liar, but I don't think he killed Clarence Stembridge. I haven't been out to check on his trip to the farm equipment business, but if he was there when he said, that's out, too."

"So where are we now?" Hillman asked.

"The remaining suspects, or even a total stranger we know nothing about. I remember the street person who was belligerent, but In reply to: have no idea where he might be. Don't know anything about him. Actually, I'd rather dismissed him as a suspect. He'd have nothing to gain other than revenge for misplaced anger."

"Sometimes that's enough, but I agree he's not a likely suspect at this point. Probably nothing there to spend time on."

"Still, if I can locate him, I'll check him out. Don't want to leave any stone unturned," Kelly said.

"It appears April is not a target," the chief said, pushing back in his chair causing it to squeak. "It's been months now with no apparent attempt on her life. What do you make of that?"

"Her father is a louse and could be guilty, but I don't think he would murder her. She told Dell Stembridge he gets nothing unless he's proven innocent."

"So what do you think? Dell is innocent or just hoping to win out somehow?"

"I'm not sure. If he's guilty, he's likely just hoping to win out somehow. I gather he's pretty self-important. May think we're not able to outwit him."

"The other antique dealer...Lennet...what about him?

"At this point, many unanswered questions. He's either extremely careless about his records or he's hiding something. I have to check with his ex-wife and especially with his son. However, they are in Hawaii."

"What about the captain?"

"April said he couldn't have done it. Actually, I tend to believe she was with him at the time of her husband's murder. She didn't admit that, but she says she is sure he didn't do it."

"And you believe her?"

"Yes. Of course, I could be wrong, but she was convincing, and I have found her to be pretty open."

"I still think you're smitten, John. Better be careful, you could be misled."

Kelly flushed. "I'll be careful," he said.

"Who does that leave?"

"Aero, the captain's crazy friend, but what would be his motive? I don't know what he'd stand to gain so that's probably just a dead end. It's his connection to the captain that keeps me on his trail."

"We do need to keep all options open. Sometimes an unlikely thing turns out to be significant in some unexpected way."

"I know."

"Sorry if I sounded critical, John. I know you're working hard. Just keep turning over every leaf."

"Yes, Sir," Kelly said and stood. "I'll go make some phone calls now. I think a call to Hawaii should be next."

***

Lilly Reilly came with Marvin. They came in holding hands like sweethearts or newlyweds. April smiled at them. She hadn't known that Lilly was Chinese. April found the young woman's pretty face and a graceful walk appealing.

"Good morning," April said. "Do come in."

Marvin moved his wife slightly in front of himself. "Mrs. Stembridge, this is Lilly."

"Hello, Lilly." April said. She gestured to a table with chairs. "Let's sit over here."

"Yes, ma'am."

I understand do secretarial work." April said.

"Yes, ma'am. I finished business school and I have had one job as a private secretary. I brought my resume." She handed the envelope to April.

"Thank you," April said. She read through the one, neatly typed page signed in black ink in Lilly's handwriting.

Lilly wrote in a surprising large script. April once read large script indicated self confidence or a big ego. Lilly appeared so dainty and soft spoken. Interesting.

"I understand you wanted to move to Columbus," April said.

"Yes ma'am, I did. My parents own a Chinese restaurant in Aberdeen that, as you probably know, is not a long way from Columbus. Birmingham was too far away."

"I see," April said.

A deep blue Cadillac stopped in front of the store and a husky, blond young man stepped out.

"Oh," Lilly said, "that's Eddie. Marvin said you might need him, too."

"Perhaps," April said. She watched the handsome young man approach the building. "Was he a football player?" she asked.

"Yes, and looks the part," Marvin said. "Not like his skinny brother."

It flashed through April's mind that Eddie Reilly, stocky blond and handsome was exactly her friend Tracy Regal's type of guy. She'd had a letter from Tracy recently in which she announced she'd had a couple of bit parts in B movies but didn't know when the 'flicks' might be released. Her letter was upbeat and funny making April wish Tracy would come home for a visit.

Moments later Eddie was in the building. He smiled and walked toward April and Lilly.

"Since I know C.D. you have to be Mrs. Stembridge," he said.

"C.D.?"

"China Doll, that's what we call her," he said grinning.

"She is pretty," April said.

"Ah, yes. Mrs. Stembridge, I brought some paper work." He reached in his pocket and brought out a couple of sheets of paper. "Information about some of the courses I took relating to art as an elective, and the names, addresses and telephone numbers of references in my resume."

"I see," April said. "Do you think you'd like to work here?"

"Yes. I think I'd like it very much," Eddie said.

"Thank you, I'll let you know," April said. She wanted to hire Lilly and Eddie on the spot, but she remembered Claudine's experience and was determined to check references before committing herself.

***

The construction of April's parents' new home began. The decision was to construct it on the slight rise a distance in back of their current home and then dismantle the old house. Extensive groundwork would be done to beautify the grand new house.

Marvelous Johnson was having a great time bossing the builders around as they attempted to construct the dwelling. The trouble was, he wanted changes made that were troubling at best and unworkable at worst. The contractor called together his workers and they left in his big truck, the foreman riding with him in the cab with the others sitting in the truck bed.

When the truck arrived, April was about to leave the store for a visit to the doctor for a check up.

"I'm sorry Mrs. Stembridge," the contractor said, "but building a house for your father is impossible."

"Impossible? Why?"

"Apparently he knows nothing about construction and he demands we do his bidding."

"I'll talk to him, Mr. Pollard," April said. "I have a doctor's appointment now, but I'll drive out later and convince him to let you build according to the original plans we agreed upon."

"Could you maybe send him on a trip somewhere while we work?" Pollard asked.

April laughed. "You know that's not a bad idea. I'll send him and Mother on a vacation."

"Better make it a long one," Pollard said.

"Maybe I could send them to visit relatives somewhere."

"How about a cruise to the Greek Islands?" one of the men in the bed of the truck shouted. "That would give us a good start."

April smiled. "I'll see what I can do," she said.

***

At the doctor's office, the nurse who weighed April in said, "You look great. Only about two months to go. How do you feel?"

"Fat," April said, grinning.

"The time will pass before you know it. Better get plenty of sleep now while you can."

An hour later after leaving the doctor's office, April drove to Watsonville, arriving in late afternoon.

Her father saw her driving in and hurried to meet her. "Them sorry men left, April. You have to make them come back and get to work. They're as sorry a bunch as I ever saw! Don't know what they're doing. I have to tell them everything."

"Dad, calm down. They do know what they're doing. I've seen other houses they've built, and you have, too."

"That was other houses. This is my house!" he said shouting.

"Yours and Mother's," April said. It annoyed her that he always named everything as his, never acknowledging any ownership by her mother. For that reason, she had even considered having the house put only in her mother's name, but knowing her mother would protest, she gave up the idea.

"I'm gonna pick another contractor," he said.

"Then you'll pay for it," April said.

"Don't sass me, girl."

"I'm not sassing, Dad. Just settle down. I have a nice surprise for you and Mama. Come on in the house and we'll talk."

"What surprise? I don't like surprises."

"You'll like this one," she said.

Once they were inside the house with Flaudie Mae, April spread some travel brochures on the kitchen table. "Come here," April said, "I'm sending you two on a vacation. Call it a belated honeymoon."

"What's all that?" Flaudie Mae asked.
"Travel brochures. Pick a trip and I'll arrange it for you and Dad. You've never been outside Mississippi and Alabama. Now's your chance to travel the world," April said.
"I ain't going nowhere," Marvelous said. "I'm gotta stay here and get my house built."
"Dad, the house will be built only if you leave. It will stay a frame like it is now if you keep trying to boss the builder around."
"Where my money goes, I'm the boss," he said.
"Mother, don't you want to take a trip?" April asked.
"Whatever your dad says."
"Oh!" April cried. "I'm leaving, but not another nail goes into this building if you don't either leave or Dad stays out of the builders way." She started out of the room when her mother took her arm.
"Don't leave, baby. We'll figure something out," Flaudie Mae said. "Stay and eat supper. I've got your favorite peach cobbler in the oven."
April heard papers rustle and saw her father going through the brochures. Maybe he was finding something of interest. After all, he'd never had the opportunity to go anywhere for a vacation.

***

Kelly was finally able to arrange to meet with Helen Madison. He had not known she worked as a desk clerk at a motel and had changing hours.
"Yes," she told him, "they know I need the job, so they work me around any old way. Sometimes from one o'clock in the afternoon until midnight. Sometimes from midnight to noon the next day. Just any old way that suits them, and the pay ain't that good either."
"Sorry, Miss Madison."

"Yeah, I need a husband to support me, but it don't look like Aero's gonna get around to a wedding. My girl friend, Josie, says I'm too dang good to him and for him, but I don't see no other man hanging around waiting to take me on. I tell her I reckon one in the hand is better than a whole bush full."

"I want to ask you a few questions about Aero."

"Yeah, like what?"

"On the night of your birthday I understand he was to take you out to celebrate," Kelly said. "That was November 19th?"

"Yes, and the dirty rat didn't show up. He called me around eleven saying his car wouldn't start. If his car wouldn't start, why didn't he call me before eight o'clock?"

"I wouldn't know," Kelly said. "What do you think?"

"I think it had something to do with that Captain Redmond he's so crazy about. Just let the captain call and he's out the door, forgetting everything and everybody else."

"Do you think the captain is, as you say 'crazy about him', too?"

"Naw! I think he uses him, but you'd never get Aero to see that. Tell you what, I think if Aero don't marry me within the next six months I'm gonna dump him."

"What do you suppose Aero and the captain were doing?"

"Who knows?"

"What have they done together?" Kelly asked.

"They go to see Dugger and some old boys fight, and they've been to New Orleans."

"So they do maintain a friendship."

"One-sided. Aero seems to pay for most everything. Never has any money, and that may be why he didn't take me out. No money, plus he's at the captain's beck and call any hour of the day or night for whatever he wants."

"Where is Aero now?"

"Don't know. He hasn't called today."

"Do you know where he was on Saturday morning January 14th, the day Miss Claudine Stembridge was shot?"

"Good Lord, you don't think he did that, do you?"

"I'm not suggesting he did, but I'm in the process of investigating. Do you know where he was that morning?"

"He said he was going to see a doctor because he was having trouble sleeping, but I don't know if that's true. Seems like he sleeps like a drunken hog when he's here."

"He drinks a lot?"

"Yes, but even when he's not drinking, I don't see a sleeping problem. He tried to quit drinking after his brother was killed, but I guess he just couldn't."

"So you think he may not have gone to the doctor? Who is his doctor?"

"Hillman or something like that. Don't really remember."

"Got a phone book?"

"Yes. Just a minute." She left the room and returned with a telephone book.

Kelly turned through to the list of physicians and came across the name 'Hillerman.' "Thanks," he said, "I see there is a similar name."

"Gosh, I hope Aero isn't in trouble."

"You care about him."

"He can be...sometimes he's dear. If he hurts my feelings he always says he's sorry. Sometimes he even cries. He just can't stand for any hard feelings between him and people he cares about, but he can't seem to juggle his time to please everybody, certainly not for me. I know why. He knows I'll be soft and forgive him without making much of a big deal of it 'cause I don't like to see him upset."

"An emotional guy then."

"Yeah, he sure is," Helen said, "but I need to stand my ground more and I aim to. You want me to tell him you came looking for him?"

"Not necessarily. I'll look him up," Kelly said.

"I'll tell him so he won't be surprised."

"All right. Thanks for your time," Kelly said.

In driving back to the police station, Kelly wondered about the information he'd uncovered. It appeared Aero might have had the time to be the killer, but why would he? Would he go that far if Redmond asked him to? The deaths allowed the fortune to fall to April, and if Redmond divorced his wife...it appeared to be a possibility. Still, what would Aero get from it? Surely just approval from Redmond wouldn't be sufficient for such a serious matter. Kelly speeded up. First things first. He'd go by Dr. Hillerman's office to check out that appointment.

Kelly parked his car and hurried into Dr. Hillerman's office. The waiting area was full of patients. Some were turning pages of magazines, others simply waiting, while some sat with their eyes closed. A busy doctor no doubt. At the receptionist desk, Kelly showed his credentials and asked if Aero Laston was a patient.

The receptionist turned to her computer and typed in the name. "Yes, Sir, he is, but he hasn't been in for over a year. Did you need to talk with Dr. Hillerman?"

"No, thanks. You're sure Mr. Laston hasn't been in for over a year?"

"Yes, sir. The date is right here."

"Very well. Thanks."

On his drive to the police station, Kelly felt excited. While he couldn't see how Aero would benefit, he thought there was enough information to see him as a real suspect. He would discuss it with the chief at once.

Chief Hillman listened with interest. "What I think we need to do next, John, is have the plain clothes tail him. Mason and Carl could switch off watches to keep from arousing suspicion. I think they should also go to Dugger's fights and sit as close to the suspect as possible...changing nights. Some overheard conversation might be helpful. At the same time, don't forget your other suspects. This is not, as you know, a done deal

Chapter Ten

April's mother called to say they'd made a choice. "Your dad wants to go to England and Germany to see where his father was during WWII."

"Great. I'll get the arrangements made with the travel agency and Mama, you come into town and I'll help you shop for some new clothes."

"You're doing so much for us. Can you really afford all this?"

"Oh, yes, and I want to do it."

"Honey, it's getting close to time for the baby. I don't want to be away then," Flaudie Mae said.

"Don't worry about it. I think you'll be back in plenty of time. I want you to have a good trip. Enjoy yourself."

"I was surprised he chose to see where his Dad had been. You know his parents worshiped the ground he walked on, but he wasn't thoughtful of them," Flaudie Mae said.

"I remember Granny being angry about that. She said Dad was so inconsiderate he needed to have a good dose of 'doing unto others as he'd have them do unto him.' He never seemed to think of their feelings. She also said they were casting their pearls before a fat hog.' I suppose it's an understatement to say Granny didn't care much for Dad," April said smiling.

"Yes, but after his parents were gone, I believe he wished he'd been more considerate. He really missed them. I had always reminded him of their birthdays, Mother's Day and Father's Day, but he wouldn't even call them. He didn't even shop for the presents they received."

"I know. You bought them for him and even delivered them yourself."

"Well, now for some reason he wants to see where his dad was during the war so that's the trip we chose," Flaudie Mae said.

"Come on into Columbus tomorrow, Mama, and we'll go shopping."

"What time?"

"Come in around eleven and we'll have lunch first," April said.

When her mother agreed and hung up, April decided to check references on her applicants. To her relief and considerable satisfaction, all references spoke well of the Reilly family. Only one notation she considered a bit significant. Eddie Reilly had so much appeal to young women that he would receive excessive telephone calls. April decided Lilly should answer the telephone and take messages for him. Lilly would know orders were often called in, and the phone should not be tied up with personal calls. True, Eddie was attractive, but she didn't intend his personal calls to interfere with business. Anyway, she didn't think blond Eddie was as handsome as John Kelly with his gray-blue eyes and dark hair. Behavior now meant more to her than looks, and Kelly had been much nicer lately. Mitchell crossed her mind for a moment, but his appeal had faded along with his lies and hateful words.

***

Late in the afternoon, when he arrived, Helen told Aero the detective had been to see her. She saw his eyes widen, and he took in a quick breath.

"What did you tell him?" Aero asked.

"Nothing much."

"What exactly?"

"That you were friends with the Air Force captain and that you didn't take me out on my birthday like you promised."

" You told him that? That was none of his business. Why did you have to tell him I couldn't make it on your birthday?"

"I don't know. We was just talking. I asked if you was in trouble."

"And what did he say?"

"I think he said 'no'."

"You 'think' he said 'no.' You don't remember?" He pressed.

"You don't remember a lot of stuff yourself, Aero. How about my roses you promised to set out for me? They're still soaking in buckets out back. I'd do it myself except you know my weak heart."

"What else did that detective say? What else did you tell him?" Aero stood close to her now, his arms akimbo and his face flushed.

Helen saw he was upset. Better cool it, she thought. "Oh, it was just nothing, Aero. He didn't stay but a few minutes."

"Watch your mouth when he comes around, Helen."

"You're making a big deal of nothing," She said.

"I don't like him snooping around. Why didn't he ask me directly?"

"He tried, but you was always out of pocket. Weeks ago he even went to the looney place to see you, but missed you there, too."

"You mean I can't be found."

"Well, you know, you and the captain spend a lot of time together," she said.

"And I suppose you told him that, too."

"Yeah, I did. So what's the problem? It's the truth. He ain't your brother, Aero, I hope you finally got that out of your brain."

"I told you never to speak against Jimbo," he said. His face grew red.

"I didn't even mention his name."

"I know what you meant," he said.

"I didn't mean anything. I thought you were better and knew the difference," she said.

"I think you run your mouth too much," he said

"Just forget it, Aero. Stop getting so emotional!"

"I don't forget Jimbo."

"Jimbo is dead and Mitchell Redmond is not Jimbo. Why can't you get that in your brain?"

"I told you never to put down Jimbo." He began working his lips into pouts like a small boy.

"I didn't," she said.

"I know what you meant. I got the message," he said, standing close to her, frowning, looking into her face.

"Oh, shut up!" she said, "Just shut up! I think you need to be back in the looney bin."

"I'll shut you up!" he said striking her hard across her mouth with the back of his hand. She fell backward against the brick fireplace and collapsed with blood tricking from her nose.

He took hold of her wrist and jerked her forward. "Get up!" he yelled.

She fell forward against his arm.

"Helen!" he cried, "Don't do that! Get up!" He gathered her up in his arms. "Don't do that. Wake up! Come on now." He propped her against the sofa. "I know," he said, "I'll get some cold water and a rag to bathe your face. Yes, then you'll wake up."

He ran to the kitchen, but after a second thought, turned around and ran into the bathroom. He grabbed a bath cloth and wet it sopping with cold water. In the bathroom mirror he glanced at his stricken face and cried out. What had he done? He ran back to Helen and bathed her face with the cold, wet rag calling out to her, demanding she wake up. He picked her up and stood her on her feet, but she fell against him like a rag doll. "I know," he said. "She needs to rest. It's her weak heart. I'll put her to bed. Yeah, that'll do it. By morning she'll be just fine." He carried her limp body to bed, undressed her and slipped her gown on. "Did I see her eyelid flicker?" he asked hopefully. "Tomorrow she'll be just fine."

He shucked off his shoes and undressed. Once in the bed he pulled her next to his bare body trying to believe she would be helped by his warmth. "There, there," he said, soothingly. "You'll be just fine."

After an hour or more he fell asleep. Around midnight he awoke and called to her. "Helen, are you awake? Wake up. I want to talk to you. Why are you so ... cold?"

He ran his hand across her face and felt the stickiness of the blood. "Oh, oh, oh," he cried. He reached to the lamp at the bedside table and gasped when he saw her face. "Helen, I...I...never meant to," he whispered. He took her hand and kissed it over and over again as he sobbed calling out her name.

He got out of bed and went to the bathroom and washed the blood from his hands. Outside the window, he saw it was dark with only pale moonlight casting shadows. He knew he had to do something, but what? He went back to the bed and gazed at her again. She could not stay there. Could he bury her out in her backyard? Then say she went to visit her sister in Arizona? Or maybe say nothing. Yes, say nothing unless asked when she didn't show up for work. Actually, she had no sister, and maybe they'd find that out.

He slipped back into his clothes and went outside to dig her grave. He knew from doing previous yard work for her where the tools were. Now where to bury her body? The rose bushes brushed against his leg as he lifted the shovel from the little shed. Yes! That was it. He'd dig the grave where she'd wanted her rose garden and then set the rose bushes out on top.

With no rain for weeks, the ground was hard. He grabbed the water hose and laid it on the ground. Maybe if he let it run for an hour he could dig easier. He opened the spigot full force and returned to the house.

He pulled down the sheet and looked at Helen's still face. He moaned and covered his face with his hands. If only she would open her eyes and speak to him! But he knew that would never happen again. He felt a sore need to share his pain with someone, but there was no one. Helen had been that someone. Mitchell would only be angry.

He moved away from the bed and sat in the rocking chair. Although it was relatively warm in the room, he felt chilled as he rocked and wept. It occurred to him he was always the giver, buying what love he could get. Helen had been the exception...putting up with him, helping him, and even loving him. It hardly seemed worthwhile to continue his life, but he feared death. He thought briefly of his male sex partners, but he knew them all to be fickle. He didn't care for them on a permanent basis, either. Mitchell was the only one he really wanted.

At seven minutes after three a.m., he left the rocker and went outside to dig the grave. He dug through the mud letting the water continue to run. Shovel after shovel he dug until he hit something like rock. The shovel couldn't cut through. Had he hit a slab of rock? He went inside the house for a flashlight.

The city waterline. Probably the hole was deep enough anyway, but he widened it to be sure. He returned to the house and packed a bag with four dresses, a gown and three sets of underwear, two pairs of shoes, a raincoat and her makeup from the bathroom and oh...get her purse. He opened the purse and took out her billfold. Forty dollars. He removed it and some change from the bottom of the purse and put it in his pocket. Not that he wished to steal it, but he reasoned it would simply be wasted otherwise.

Outside once again, he put the bag in the hole first, then returned for her body. He wrapped her in the bloody sheets and the comforter from the bed and carried her to the grave. Daylight was breaking so he hurriedly shoveled in the muddy dirt. Oh, the rose bushes! He gathered them up and set them out as quickly as he could. Once more he turned on the water hose to wash down the area. He put the hose back, neatly circled and hung over the hook the way Helen always wanted it done.

Back inside the house, he cleaned up the blood from the hearth, turned over the blood-stained mattress, and spread the bed up in neat order with clean sheets and a bedspread before leaving. Now no one would ever know, if he could bear that lump in his chest alone.

He hurriedly entered his old black Ford and drove, lights off, down the hill onto the roadway. He planned when he reached his apartment to take a shower, down two sleeping pills and go to bed. But before that—the razor.

Chapter Eleven

April saw the mail carrier approaching the house. She had hoped for a postcard from her mother, but none had come. Ten days into their European trip and no word. Well, maybe today. She rushed down the stairs and to the front door.

"Did I get a card, Samuel?"

"Nope. I know you been looking for a card, but here's a letter. Will that do?" The big man grinned as he handed her the letter on top of her other mail.

"Yes!" April said. "It's from Mama."

"Better than a card," Samuel said.

"Much!" April said. "Thanks a bunch."

"I don't write 'em. I just deliver 'em, but glad you got it. Good day," he said and shuffled down the steps on his way.

April closed the door and sat on the bench in the entryway to open her mail. She heard footsteps and looked up.

"The mail come?" Mary Jean asked.

"Yes, and there's a letter from Mama." April tore open the envelope.

"What she say?" Mary Jean asked. "She okay?"

April read quickly. She laughed. "Oh, my Dad is something else! Mama said he says the people in England don't speak good English. They talk funny, he says. But he has been interested in seeing places his father mentioned. No museums or castles, though. He prefers to sit in the park and watch people. I suspect he hopes to see pretty girls pass by."

"How soon they be coming home?" Mary Jean asked.

"In about three weeks. I arranged a longer trip than Dad wanted, but the builders needed the time. Oh, here's a letter from my friend who went to Hollywood." April looked up at Mary Jean. "She...Tracy Regal, and I were best friends in high school. She was fun...such a scatterbrain." April quickly read

Tracy's letter. "She's getting a screen test for a part in a new movie. Good...sure hope she gets it. Says she doesn't know when she'll get back home."

"Ma'am, you had a call from a Captain Redmond. He said he would call back later."

April's heart skipped a beat. She wanted to hear his voice and see his amazing face. *What kind of fool am I after all he's done?* She set her lips in a firm line. "When he calls, Mary Jean," April said, "Tell him I'm not accepting personal calls from the Air Force. Just that. Let him think whatever he wants." April smiled. She felt proud of herself for being strong when she felt so tempted. Would he keep calling? Could she hold out? She absolutely must!

Upstairs in her bedroom she took out the group picture that included him. She sighed. Why did he have to be so handsome? Why did she have to be such a fool over handsome men? She reminded herself of the pain he'd caused her and that he was married. Another glance at his face and she started to rip apart the picture. After a tiny tear at the edge, she sighed and stopped. She returned the photograph to her dresser drawer. Maybe later. After all, the picture was not actually him.

***

The call to Kelly from the police detective in Hawaii came at last. Nealeana Lennet Woodfield had been located. The detective said at first she denied her son was there, apparently afraid someone might come to take him away. When she understood Daw was not in trouble, she admitted he had arrived at her home two days before, but was not there at the moment. He and his step-father, Keaton, had gone fishing.

"Have him call me collect," Kelly said. "Let's try for tomorrow at ten o'clock in the morning your time. I should be back in the office by then."

Next day, as planned, Daw called. The first thing he said was, "I ain't coming back."

"I'm not asking you to come back," Kelly said. "I just want to ask you a few questions."

"Like what?"

"Where you and your father were Saturday night, November the nineteenth?"

"November the nineteenth? Shoot, how would I know that?"

"You might remember. It was the night Mr. Stembridge was murdered," Kelly said.

"We had nothing to do with that! I don't know where we were. That was months ago."

"Think back. You must have heard of it the next day. What did you do that day?"

"I don't know. All I know is I didn't do it and I don't think he did either. Now Dugger could have, but he had no reason to."

"Why do you mention Dugger then?" Kelly asked.

"Because he had killed somebody before he came to Columbus. It was in the wrestling ring, but he sure didn't seem to be sorry about it. He just said, 'Everybody gotta die sometime.' "

"But you mentioned him in connection to Mr. Stembridge."

"Like I said, he had no reason. Now if somebody had paid him a chunk of change, I reckon he wouldn't have minded to do the job."

"He'd kill for money?"

"I've heard him say, 'life is filled with baloney so gittin' killed is a gift. Too bad there's a law agin it.' Still, he didn't bump himself off, and he sure likes money. Fancy wheels...that's what he loves. Did you see his new Hummer? Drive down to his shack and see that long shed he built. Got old big wheels in it."

"You're saying he'd kill for money. Do you think someone paid him to kill Mr. Stembridge?"

"Aw, I don't know. Couldn't say about that."

"Who are his friends?" Kelly asked.

"Don't reckon he has any real friends. He's basically a loner. People like to watch him fight and some wheel lovers admire his wheels, but no personal involvement that I know of."

"Have you ever seen him with anyone in particular maybe more than once?"

"Can't say that I have. Well, I seen him eat sandwiches outside the shop a few times with a street person...big guy like himself, but I think he just gave that guy part of his lunch...maybe felt sorry for him or something. Sure wouldn't been no money there. Shoot, I don't know...sometimes folks say them guys have money buried in cans...you know, turn up rich after they die or get discovered somehow."

"What's the street person's name?"

"They call him 'Juke Box Sam.' He don't actually live on the street. Lives in a old school bus. Used to work on jukeboxes, putting in the records. Over that old timey shop where they got history stuff."

"Memories?" Kelly asked.

"Yeah, that's it. But I guess you know that place shut down and I don't reckon Juke Box has a job now."

"How does he support himself?"

"Don't know. Begs, maybe steals. Don't know."

"Where does he live?"

"In a old school bus in the junk yard."

"You seem to know a lot about him."

"Some kids spray painted his 'house' purple on Halloween."

"And you went along." Kelly said.

Daw laughed. "I seen it later," he said, "but Juke Box didn't care. They coulda polka dotted it for all he'd care about that."

"A friendly good natured person?" Kelly asked.

"Naw. Looks sour and they say if you piss him off he don't forgive."

"Gets into arguments or fights?" Kelly asked.

"Gosh, I don't know. Why you asking me all this stuff?"

"Thought maybe you knew the old man better."

"I don't, but he ain't very old."

"All right. Thanks, Daw."

"Yes, Sir."

Kelly hesitated then added, "Do you have any idea who would have wanted Mr. Stembridge dead?"

"Nope, but I guess it could be anybody who wanted a chance at that store. They make a heap of money. Lots more than my old man does."

"How did your dad react to the news of Mr. Stembridge's death?"

"I think he said something like, 'His sister may be ready to sell now', and he was disappointed when she wasn't selling."

"How disappointed?"

"Not enough to kill him. He's too chicken for that. Hey, can I go now? I don't want nothing more to do with any of that stuff."

"He tried to involve you?"

"After the lady died, he wanted me to...to romance April. Gosh, imagine that. Why would she want me? Truth is, I don't want her either. I got me a girl. I aim to get her over here soon as I can."

"Where was your dad Saturday morning, January 14th, the day Miss Claudine was shot?"

"I don't know."

"Do you know a Mary Smith?"
"Mary Smith? No."
"Did you help your dad keep records of his merchandise?"
"No. He done that himself. His store and me. That was what he's been into. Like my mom says, he needs to git himself a life."
"All right. I'll let you go for now, Daw. It seems you like being in Hawaii."
"I wish I'd come to Hawaii a long time ago. I ain't never coming back to Columbus, Mississippi, and that dang antique business."
"Maybe never say 'never', but for now good bye," Kelly said and hung up. Now maybe he'd better check out Juke Box Sam. Somehow he felt irritated. Too many dead ends and probably Juke Box was just another eccentric character barely existing on handouts and stealing.

***

April dressed in a new navy blue print maternity dress with a white lace collar. She ran her hand over her now very round middle and felt a tiny kick. She smiled. Her unborn child had become a reality to her. About six weeks left until he or she should be born ... August 15th if the calculation was right. She glanced out the window at the beauty of the summer flowers in full bloom. A shiny, black BMW drove up and parked out front. Mitchell! She watched as he left the car. Mary Jean was away, so it was totally up to her to respond to the doorbell...or ignore it.

She watched. He was so handsome in full uniform as he strode toward the front door. She put her hand over her heart. *Don't answer the door! Leave! Go out the back door. Get in your car and go! No, don't be foolish. Just don't answer the door.* She sat in the rocker in her room. The one she meant to use to rock her baby in, but she let the doorbell ring unanswered.

She continued to sit after the insistent ringing of the doorbell ceased. Memories of their time together filled her thoughts. She'd never been so happy. He had seemed so perfect...so exciting. Surely their romance would have continued, had she not become pregnant. Still she remembered the pain when he hurt her with those terrible words! Now, in a sense, she was thankful for that pain. It made it easier for her to resist him. Why had he reappeared? Why? A change of heart? What about his marriage and his two little children? She wished they had met earlier, before he was married, and they could have been together always. Foolish dreaming. She rose abruptly from the rocker and walked to the dresser to make one last touch to her lipstick.

She was now ready to go to the store. Once more she glanced out the window to make sure he was gone. Would he return? Probably. Maybe next time she'd find out what he was thinking. She could handle it couldn't she? Just remember his bad side.

She heard the back door whine, then close. With the security system armed it had to be either Mary Jean or Jayson.

Downstairs she met Mary Jean who fanned her face. "Very hot out there for middle May," Mary Jean said.

"I won't be out in it long...just to the car and then into the store."

"Good. Need to take care of yourself and the baby." Mary Jean smiled.

"Yes, time is drawing near. I'm more than ready to see what he or she looks like. I'm more excited about it every day. Imagine me with my own little boy or girl!"

"Bound to be a pretty young'un with you looking like you do, and if it gets them pretty blue eyes of Mr. Stembridge. I always thought the family's special blue eyes looked like a sleepy doll's I had once."

"You're sweet, Mary Jean. I always feel good when you're around."

"Thank you ma'am."

"Well, I'll be going now. See you later," April said.

Outside, she was surprised. Mitchell drove up. He lowered the car window and called to her. "April, I want to talk to you," he said. "Come get in the car. It's too hot out there."

"I don't have time." She spoke abruptly.

"This won't take long, honey. Please, just a little time and I'll leave," he said.

She hesitated, but then went to his car. He pushed open the door for her to enter. When she was inside, he reached to kiss her but she resisted.

"Wow," he said, "you really hate me, don't you?"

"What do you want?" she asked without looking at him.

"Sweetheart, we're having a baby and I intend to be with you...to be there for you at the hospital."

"No, you're not!" She said, looking at him now, frowning.

"Why?" he asked. "We can even give him my name. I'll admit paternity."

She opened the car door to leave, but he held her back. "Please," he said. "Don't leave."

"Goodbye," she said. "Go home to your family."

"What will it matter now if I claim my baby?" he asked. "Your husband and sister-in-law are no longer around."

"But I am. I won't have my baby claimed by a married man...thank you very much!"

"April, I'm going home to get a divorce. We can be married later," he said.

She was surprised at the strength of the fury rising within her. How embarrassing to have her unfaithfulness publicly revealed in this small city! The news media would be all over it, to say nothing of any legal conditions. Wouldn't Dell love it! "Don't you dare show up," she said.

He bristled. "How are you going to stop me? I have my rights," he said.

She felt frightened now. What really could she do? "Speaking of 'rights' did you ever hear of doing the right thing, Mitchell?"

"Honey, I'm trying to do the right thing by you and our child. Oh, maybe there'd be an initial fuss, since you carry a prominent name, but it'll soon die down and all will be fine."

She forcefully pushed open the door and wrenched her arm from his grasp. "You have the sensitivity of a...," she struggled for a word. " a...leech. It's all about what you want."

"What about you? You come across as so soft and tender, but underneath you're hard as nails."

"You might better remember that," she said. Hey, it felt good. She didn't know where it came from but she liked the suggestion she had power.

"All right," he said. "go on now, but I'll be back."

She slipped out, slammed the door, and went into the garage for her car. Sudden tears filled her eyes. What if he showed up at the hospital? What could she do?

***

Kelly drove to the junkyard to interview Juke Box Sam. He thought the so-called street person was an unlikely suspect, but he meant to interrogate him as he had the others.

The old, now purple, school bus parked under an oak tree by a big ditch had become the big man's home. At least, he wouldn't have to knock on the door. Juke Box was in view. He sat in a rickety lawn chair behind a small, wooden table eating from half a watermelon with a fork. Black seeds lay in a scattered pattern around him.

Kelly parked and stepped out of his car. Juke Box watching him, called out, "Private property, mister. Git going!"

Kelly removed his identification from his shirt pocket and flashed it. "Detective Kelly," he said. "I want to talk with you."

"Why? I ain't done nothing," Juke Box said. He took a bite of his nearly finished watermelon and pushed it aside.

"I'm not saying you have. I'm asking a lot of people questions, sir."

"*Sir?*" Juke Box laughed. "Ain't nobody called me 'sir' in a snake's snicker."

Kelly said, "I assume you're a gentleman."

"Gentle as a thousand leg walking on your arm."

"What's your real name? I understand Juke Box is a nickname."

"My real name? I think when I was a kid, my name on my butt bustin' report card was Sam Palms." He brushed back strands of dark, oily hair from his forehead.

"When did you stop calling yourself your real name?"

"Oh, Sam is my real name. I guess, anyway. I ran away from home after a beating when I was seven. Been on my own ever since."

"Where's your family?"

"Dead and gone to hell, I hope."

Kelly saw he appeared serious. He let the remark go and said, "I'd like to ask you a few questions, Mr. Palms."

"You done done that," Juke Box said. He laughed, revealing chunky, widely spaced yellow teeth.

"Additional questions, Mr. Palms."

"*Mr. Palms* ... now don't that sound grand?"

"All right," Kelly said, "Juke Box. Where were you on Saturday night, November the nineteenth?"

"Watching Bama put the heat on Old Miss."

"Where?"

"On TV."

"Where? What television?" Kelly asked.

"My little twelve-incher in black and white. You wanta see her?"

"Were you watching with a friend?"

"Just me and Roy."

"Roy who?"

"Roy Roach."

"Where does he live? I'd like to talk with him," Kelly said.

"Roy ain't no good at talking. He likes to finish off my supper and look at me, but talking...never heard him say a word."

"He's deaf and dumb?"

"I don't know. How do you test a roach for a thing like that?"

Kelly stared at him. "You mean we're discussing an insect?"

"Roy may be a insect to you, but he's my night buddy."

Kelly sighed. "Where were you on Saturday morning, January the fourteenth?"

"No telling. Don't have a hank of a memory for them there beans."

"You don't know where you were? Miss Claudine Stembridge was shot that morning. You probably heard about her."

"I heard, but I didn't really know the old broad. Oh, I knew who she was, but know her, like *really know* her, I never did. Can't know every old broad, you know."

"That's not very respectful."

"I heard she croaked. Well, what the heck? She had a good life. Rich. Probably ate steak and fried chicken any time she pleased. Older than me. Well, the places she bought stuff probably been missing her."

"Did you shoot her?"

"Heck, no! I ain't a good shot. Miss ever dang rabbit I ever try to kill."

"I see. Can anyone verify where you were on that day?

Juke Box scratched his head. "Now how could I say? I don't remember myself. Probably, I was just going through my old records. You know some of them is probably gonna be worth something some day. I got Elvis and lots of others."

Kelly mumbled, "Sure." He dropped his head. What a screwed up interview! The man was worse than Matton Lennet...or was he simply losing his skill as an investigator?

Juke Box said. "If you happen to pass this way anytime, you could drop me off some Colonel Sanders. I like original recipe. The crunchy type kinda hurts my teeth."

Kelly walked to his car, got in and slammed the door.

" 'Sir'! 'Mr. Palm,' that's my good'uns for the day," Juke Box said. He laughed, picked up his watermelon rind, scooped out one more bite and tossed it aside. He got up and went inside to turn on his little twelve-incher to watch some Jerry Springer.

Chapter Twelve

April was pleased to find all three employees busy when she arrived at her antique store. Not that she needed the money, but simply that she'd been able to do what she believed Clarence and Claudine would have wanted.

She waved and smiled at them, and took a seat near the front window. Outside she watched a little girl walking along the sidewalk. The child had on a green-checkered dress and her auburn hair was in pigtails. She cuddled a gray kitten under her chin, causing April to reflect on her own, very different childhood. Dad hated all cats so she was never allowed to have a kitten. He called them all females. April thought it fit for his way of thinking. She'd always known that he would have preferred for her to have been born a boy. At least, his dear hounds were male.

"Telephone, Mrs. Stembridge," Lilly called.

"Telephone? All right, be right there." Maybe Mary Jean needed something from the grocery.

No! It was Mitchell again! "Don't hang up," he said. "I'm going home tomorrow on a short leave. When I get back I'll be on my way to being a free man."

"Goodbye, Mitchell,"

"April, I'm going to get a divorce."

"Not for me."

"Now, sweetheart, don't be that way. I love you."

"You don't know what love is, Mitchell Redmond!"

"April, for crying out loud! You know what we had...what we can have in the future. I'm going home to start the divorce like I'm promising you."

"I repeat. Not for me."

"What has happened to you? I want to be with you and our son."

"Could be a girl, Mitchell, but she'll be a Stembridge."
"Legally, maybe until the DNA."
Oh, God! She'd not thought of that. She felt faint.
"I'll see you when I get back." He hung up the phone.

***

Kelly waited outside the chief's office until the mayor left. Wonder what business they had? Maybe nothing related. He slumped down in the bench outside the office. This whole Stembridge murder was getting to him. Or maybe it was simply that he was embarrassed he had nothing significant to report. Well, everybody knew it sometimes took years to solve murders, if they were ever solved at all.

The mayor left the chief's office with a pleasant expression on his face, so all must have gone well, whatever it was. Kelly saw the chief look in his direction and motion him in.

He nodded, walked in and slid into his usual seat.

"You look gloomy, John," the chief said. "Got a problem?"

"Just let me tell you about the interview I just had with this Juke Box fella."

"Got something there?" the chief asked and sat up with a hopeful expression on his face.

Kelly told him the details.

"Hummmm," the chief said. "I think he's a lot more clever than we might give him credit for. Think about making it on his own since he was seven, assuming that's true, but look at what else we have here. He knew about the exact ballgame and he thinks little of human life. He claims to be a poor shot and Miss Claudine was only wounded when she was fired on. Maybe I'm making too much of this, but see where I'm coming from?"

"I do," Kelly said, and he felt inadequate that he hadn't put it together. He didn't want to admit it.

"Did you see it that way, John?"

Better not lie. "Frankly, no, Chief, I have to admit I didn't. I found the man so irritating with all the spinning he did in his talk I didn't see it clearly. Still, I do remember he had an angry run-in with Clarence Stembridge when he wasn't given as much money as he wanted. Must feel entitled to gifts and hostile when he doesn't get what he wants, but angry enough to kill...don't know."

"I'm glad you interviewed him. You're doing a good job, John. You turn over all the stones and it's damn frustrating the way things go many times."

Kelly smiled. He felt better now. Maybe he'd go check on April to see if Dell was bothering her or if her dad was back putting on the pressure.

When Kelly left the office he remembered Juke Box hadrequested he drop him off some Colonel Sanders original recipe. Requested or *ordered*? Kelly smiled. Let him dream!

***

Aero reached home just before daybreak. He climbed to his third story apartment making as little noise as possible. He looked down at the cement parking lot below and considered jumping down headfirst. Always when he did really bad things, he thought of suicide first. Helen said when he was sent to the Looney Bin, the drugs and alcohol was killing him. The psychiatrist agreed, but at least that method had put him out of his misery for periods of time. Coward that he was, he never could quite make the final step. As he saw it, the world was good and bad. Helen was good. He was bad. Mitchell was beautiful. He was ugly. Crime was bad. Punishment was good.

When he tried to put the key in the lock, his hand shook. He clasped one hand over the other to steady the trembling. Once inside his apartment, he prepared himself for his punishment. He felt bad about not jumping to the parking lot and ending his worthless life, but the very thought of Mitchell kept him from it.

He went to the bathroom, took the barber razor from the cabinet and removed his shirt. He closed the lid on the commode and sat down. Slowly, he nicked his forearm until it was a sheet of blood. Was that enough? Maybe better do some on the other arm. The pain stung like fire, but he was careful not to cut too deep. Now, maybe that would do. He dabbed the blood until the flow stopped, then reached for his jar of Vaseline. He smeared a thick coat over the wounds and opened the linen cabinet. A ragged old white sheet tumbled out. He tore off strips and wrapped both arms. He'd need to set the alarm to get to work by dark. Let's see, three minutes after 6:00 AM now.

He went into the kitchen, pushed a piece of bread in the toaster, poured leftover coffee in a pan on the stove and heated it. After he choked down the bite of breakfast, he went into the bedroom, turned the clock dial to 5:00 PM, pulled up the alarm button and slipped into his rumpled bed. Helen's sheets were always clean, but he didn't fool with his. Sometimes she came over and changed them. She always fussed at him about such things as clean sheets and towels.

In bed, he wept briefly thinking of Helen in her grave. He turned his thoughts to Mitchell and back to Helen. She had told him repeatedly that Mitchell was using him unmercifully. "Stop being the fool," she'd said, but he couldn't. She thought he believed Mitchell was Jimbo, but that had changed during the past year. Now he saw Mitchell as a flawlessly handsome male whom he wanted to love him. A few times when they were fully clothed, Mitchell had hugged him, and when they'd gone to New Orleans, he'd seen him in the shower. But touching was off limits. He'd had to worship him from afar.

Helen nagged about it...kept asking him when he was going to realize he was being played the fool. "Think about what happened in New Orleans," she'd said. She had a point for sure. In New Orleans he had to pay for everything and when they went to Antoine's he was short on cash. Mitchell frowned and jerked his chair back, prepared to leave the restaurant. To appease Mitchell, he'd overloaded his credit card and then worried all through the night about how he'd pay his bills.

That night in New Orleans, tossing and turning in the wee hours, he knew he needed to get Mitchell Redmond out of his life. But he remembered a promise Mitchell had made him. "One day you're going to be really happy you've helped me, Aero," Mitchell had told him. Mitchell often repeated that statement, but he wouldn't say why or when ... only, "I won't spoil the secret." Not even a hint. Helen had said, "Press him for *when*?" But Mitchell wouldn't budge. She said, "He's holding out a carrot you'll never get. Honey, it's N and N...never and nothing." But Helen didn't know. She was guessing. Maybe there was something really special for him if he could be patient.

Tonight, he couldn't go to sleep so he got up and took two pain pills. Maybe if his arms quit hurting, and if he could stop thinking over every detail, he could relax. He walked around and around the room for at least a half hour. First he felt too cold and then too hot. He knew he was exhausted and forced himself back to bed. He lay on his back until he was miserable with the position. When he turned over, he felt relieved and fell asleep.

***

Dell Stembridge emptied coins from a jar onto his kitchen table. Short of April coming through or making a loan on his property, which he resisted, he was virtually penniless. He'd even been picking up cans off the highway and around town for the few coins it would bring. That was embarrassing, so he took them to a little out of the way store to collect the pay.

He left his house and walked the three quarters of a mile to Burger Palace. His three-year-old Cadillac held about two gallons of gasoline, and he was saving it for an emergency. At home, he could have had a peanut butter and jelly sandwich, but he wanted a burger, and he wanted to see Faith Ann. They'd smiled and held lingering eye contact since the first day. Then they'd started having brief conversations. If he had the money he'd have asked her out on a date. He hated being so damn poor! Maybe he should get a loan on the house and try his luck at the casino again. But he had a real attachment to the old home place now. It was his only real link to his Stembridge heritage and he thought being a Stembridge property owner gave him status.

He yanked open the restaurant door expecting to see the cute brunette with the turned up nose and big, brown eyes, but she was not in sight. "Where's Faith Ann?" he asked.

"She had to take her mother to the doctor," the skinny young boy said.

"When will she be back, Casey?"

"Don't know. She and her mom live by theyselves, and I think Mrs. Hogan is kinda sickly."

"Well, damn," Dell said. Why couldn't the woman get somebody else to take her to the doctor? He wanted to see Faith Ann.

"Wanta order?" Casey asked.

"Yeah. Give me a burger, extra tomato and lettuce," Dell said. "I'll just drink some water."

"Faith Ann won't be here much next week," the boy offered. "She's helping out with the kids in Vacation Bible School."

Dell frowned. Gosh, she was into religion. Granddad used to take him to church when he was a kid, but he hadn't been in years. And he had not one ounce of interest in it. Better just forget her.

He ate his burger and gulped the water. Wonder if he could sell that patch of pines back of the house? Maybe some pulpwood man would be interested. Damn April! He didn't want to keep waiting while Kelly kept puttering around. If Kelly was so smart, why hadn't he figured it out? He wasn't smart enough, that's why. Small city detective, that's all he was. April might as well give him the money. Kelly was never gonna solve it. Never.

Dell sat studying his problem and thumping the saltshaker around. He needed that money now. Still, if he could sell the pines, he'd have some cash to gamble on. Could have a change in his luck and win big. Sometimes it did happen. He crunched together the wrapper from his burger and his paper cup but didn't bother to toss them into the bin on the way out. Casey could do that.

As he walked toward home he decided he would press April to set a deadline. Like if the murder hadn't been solved in a year, he'd get his money. It had already been nearly a year..well, not quite. April's kid hadn't been born yet, but it was getting close to time.

Immediately after he walked in the door back home, he called the agriculture department to ask questions about finding timber cutters for small plots. Nobody had an answer. He slammed the phone down in disgust.

Maybe if he called April, she'd give him some money in advance. He'd ask her. First he called the store and then her home.

"April, this is Dell," he said. "Look we're family, you know, and I'm...well, I'm in bad need of some cash. How about a small advance...say ten thousand...or maybe just five?"

April sighed. "Dell, you know what the condition is for my giving you money. Besides, I don't intend to have you waste any money gambling."

"April, it's not that. You see, I've met this girl...a fine Christian girl. I want to go to church with her and be able to put something in the collection plate."

"You're dating?"

"Yes, and when we go to church I don't want to look cheap.. I'm down to my last coins, so I can't even take her out any more, or I wouldn't have called you."

"Sorry, but you have to prove a thing or two first."

"April! Have mercy!"

"You need to learn something my Granny told me, Dell. Your reputation follows you like your shadow."

"I'm not gambling now," he said.

"Of course not, but what if you did have the money? I'm not going to contribute to keeping you a weak person, Dell. Proof first, just like I said. Besides, the murder hasn't been solved yet."

"That small time detective is never going to solve anything. Be reasonable, for Pete's sake, April. Set a deadline. How about if he hasn't solved it in a year?"

"Forget that."

Dell sighed heavily. "You're one hard-hearted woman, April. We're family and you're not treating me right. I'm so worried I can't sleep and I can barely afford to eat and what I do eat is ruining my health."

"Poor Dell! I heard how you worked your family with pitiful tales. It was to your detriment. You're not working me." April said.

He moaned. "Check my closed bank account. Check my piggy bank. You'll see I have nothing but coins. It's a lonely peanut butter sandwich for supper and then my cupboard will be bare."

April said. "Proof, Dell, and solid promises. A one time gift when the time comes ... if it comes, and then you'd better manage or you'll be right back where you are now. Goodbye."

"Hey, wait! I tried to find out how I could sell this patch of pine in the field back of the house, but nobody seems to know who'd be interested."

"Dad would know, and they'll be back from Europe tomorrow. I'll ask him and tell you what he says. It may be that would bring you in some money...but not to throw away, I hope."

"No way! I've got to please Faith Ann and she's not into gambling."

"You have a sensible girl friend? Well, congratulations, for one step in the right direction. I'll call you when I find out," April said and hung up.

She sat then for a while reflecting on Granny and her life lessons.

Although, he didn't know it, Dell was being blessed by her guilt over her own behavior with Mitchell Redmond. Otherwise, she might not have considered giving him a second chance...assuming, of course, he was not the family murderer.

Chapter Thirteen

Aero awoke at five p.m. with the ringing of his alarm clock. At first he punched off the alarm and turned over, still feeling sleepy. Then he remembered and sat up, as reality dawned upon him. Oh, how one night had changed his life! Now what would happen next? His one true friend was gone. He covered his face with both hands. Never had he felt so vulnerable. And he would be asked about her when she didn't show up. Would it be best to say she went to visit friends he didn't know...somewhere out in Colorado? Or should he simply claim not to know? Lots of people knew they were often together. Probably better to claim she was in Colorado. But when she didn't appear ever ... what then?

He got out of bed and went to the kitchen and put coffee on. His stomach felt queasy, but he thought he should eat something. Maybe boil a couple of eggs to avoid grease from frying. After he put the eggs on he went to the freezer and took down the loaf of bread. Helen had told him to freeze it to keep it fresh and then toast it. He had been putting it in the refrigerator where it dried out before he could use it. She'd been like a mother in that way...looking after him, advising him. He dropped in a kitchen chair at the table and sobbed. Soon, however, it occurred to him he needed to stop weeping and pull himself together. Somehow he must appear well and cheerful at work. He went to the sink and splashed cold water on his face.

Only later, when he was driving to work, did he remember something else of great importance. Helen had made a will leaving him her home and all of her assets ... such as they were. He remembered the day when she told him and he had protested. "What about your family?"

"I have no family," she'd said. "There were few of us to begin with, and my people didn't live into old age. Probably I won't either." She'd smiled and said, "I'm the last little leaf on the Madison tree. Besides, Aero, I love you. I want you to have what I have if you outlive me. Otherwise, I'd have left it to an orphanage."

The tears came again. He pulled off the street and tried once again to collect himself. He knew he could look like a suspect in her disappearance, since he stood to gain when she never returned. Well, if they charged him and executed him, he would deserve it. He'd had plenty of times when he thought his life wasn't worth living anyhow. Still, for some crazy reason he wanted to live now...wanted to find some happiness. If only Mitchell would show him some affection, it would mean so much.

At Hector's he parked his old black Ford and took one last look in the visor mirror to check his appearance. Too pale. First thing, he'd go to the bathroom and splash cold water on his face...maybe scrub his skin with a paper towel to bring up a little color.

He saw Mitchell's BMW parked close to the front in his usual place marked 'Reserved.' Even Hector gave Mitchell special privilege. Was there something going on there? Naw. Hector, the cowboy, was too much of a John Wayne. Maybe it was just because Mitchell helped to draw the crowd and that was business.

The whole nightclub, even the restroom, reflected Hector's love of the old West. The walls were decorated with cowboy boots and chaps that had seen better days. Mexican lanterns hung from the ceilings and provided soft but adequate illumination. Aero found the restroom empty and was grateful for the privacy. A panel of mirrors allowed him a relatively clear view of his reflection.

He had only wet his hands when Mitchell walked in. After one glance, Mitchell asked, "What the hell is wrong with you?"

***

Jayson picked up April's parents at the airport to save her the trip on the very hot July 14th. Marvelous was eager to get on home to see how "his" new house looked but he also wanted something to eat. Mary Jean had a meal almost ready when they arrived. The mingled aromas of fried chicken, sweet potatoes, fried okra, and chocolate pie, drifted from the kitchen.

Marvelous said, "That sure smells good. Home at last."

"It is good to be home," Flaudie Mae said, "but April, I really enjoyed the tour. So many beautiful and interesting places."

Marvelous said, "You can't eat the scenery. Them folks across the pond don't know a thing about cooking. I nearly starved."

April smiled. "Really, Dad? Then how did you put on those extra pounds?"

"I had to eat. I didn't say I didn't eat, but they sure can't cook like your ma can."

"A compliment, Mama," April said and saw her mother smile.

"Yeah," Marvelous said, "Your ma ain't much to look at, but she's a Miss America when it comes to puttin' a spread on the table."

"Dad, I wish you wouldn't say hateful things about Mama's looks. She's beautiful in every way that counts."

"Oh, I know. I married her, didn't I? I knew what I was doing when I saw what a good one she was at getting up early and staying steady with the chores until they was done."

April sighed. "You should be ashamed, Dad."

"Why?"

"Never mind. She's not going to work so hard from now on. I'm opening her own bank account and she can hire any help she pleases," April said.

"Her own bank account. Naw. I handle the money."

"You'll have your bank account and she'll have hers and don't you dare try to talk her out of it or your account will not get a penny richer over time."

He frowned. "Getting all that money has made a smartie out of you, girl."

April grinned. "Thanks," she said and then changed the subject, "Dell Stembridge has a small grove of pine trees he wants cut, but he doesn't know who to contact. You do, don't you, Dad? Didn't you used to work in timber?"

"Yeah, sure did. He'll have a choice of the professor or Jubal Boy Jenkins."

"How would he know which one to contact?"

"If he wants to understand his trees, have each one chose for cutting, and if he wants to learn about beetles that can kill 'em, he should phone up the professor. If he just wants the suckers clear cut, Jubal Boy is his man."

"I doubt he'll want to be educated, but I'll ask him. By the way, who is the professor?"

"He's this black dude, Ezekiel Jones, who got all educated up. Had a job down at Ole Miss making the professor bucks until last year." Marvelous stretched and yawned before continuing. "Age caught up with him, but he set hisself up a local timber cutting business. Hired a couple of big old boys to do the labor. But Ezekiel hisself chooses and marks the trees to be cut, leaving seed trees for the next crop."

"That sounds very sensible, but Dell may just want as much money as he can get. Is Jubal Boy responsible..honest?"

"Ah, he's just a dumb old boy who cuts everything to the ground."

"What do you think, Dad? Who would you choose and what would be the difference in the payout?"

"The man would come out better with the professor if he wants another growth in a few years, but he'd get more money from Jubal Boy."

"Because all the trees would be cut?"

"Yeah."

"Thanks, Dad. You know you can be pretty smart at times."

"Just at times?"

"At times," April said, laughing.

Mary Jean appeared. "Telephone, Mrs. Stembridge. It's that captain."

"Tell him I'm busy," April said.

"Yes, ma'am. The food is ready when you all want to eat," she said.

"Who is the captain?" Marvelous asked. "You got a boy friend?"

"No. Not now," April said.

"Well, who is he?" Marvelous persisted.

"Someone I used to date, but he's history now."

"Don't sound like it to me," Marvelous said. "You better be careful, girl. He may be after *our* money."

"I can handle him," April said, but a moment of panic rose in her. The money aside the DNA was another matter. Could he demand that legally?

***

Faith Ann parked her five-year-old bright blue Chevrolet in front of the Burger Castle. Before she left her car, she saw something that surprised her...Dell Stembridge putting some soft drink cans in a grocery bag at the side of the building. She'd thought he had money. Weren't all the Stembridges' rich? He lived in a grand old house. So what was he doing? She had noticed he always paid for his burger with coins and seldom bought a soda. She knew he was attracted to her but he'd never asked her out. For some reason he must have a financial problem, but why? She opened the door to her car and got out. Maybe she'd make the first move and see what happened.

When he came inside he set his grocery bag in a booth and went to order. "Hi Faith Ann," he said, "I've been missing you."

"I've needed to be away a few times," she said. "How are you?"

"I'm okay. Guess I'll have a burger, lots of tomato and lettuce," he said.

"Sure," she said, "I know how you like it." She punched the order in the computer. "Anything to drink?"

"Water," he said.

"Dell," she said, "would you think me too forward if I asked you to join Mother and me Sunday? We're going about five miles from here to Pleasant Valley church for an old fashioned dinner on the ground. Those country ladies really know how to cook."

"Sure. I mean I'd like that," Dell said.

"If it doesn't interfere with your church plans...I wouldn't want to do that."

"Oh, no," Dell said. "I have no plans."

"Very well, then," she said. "I'll pick you up, because I know right where the church is out in the country. Can you be ready by around ten o'clock? We'll need to get there with our food and then, of course, there's the sermon before we eat."

"Uh huh," Dell said. He hadn't counted on a sermon, but he was really interested in the food and Faith Ann.

"I think your burger is ready," she said. She smiled. "I'm glad you can go Sunday. I think you'll enjoy it."

"Sure will," he said. He picked up his sandwich and went to the booth where his cans were. He calculated he had about three dollars worth and a bit of change at home. There would be the collection plate at church. Maybe if he wadded a couple of bucks and then folded them it would appear to be more than it was.

"See you later," he called to Faith Ann when he was ready to leave. Since she was looking at him, he dutifully carried his trash to the disposal can by the door.

When he got home, he found he had a message from April on his answering machine. He felt excited at the thought of getting his timber cut, but that wouldn't be before Sunday. Skinflint April had at least come through with names and telephone numbers he could call.

***

Aero looked at Mitchell and momentarily tried to deny anything was wrong, but tears ran down his cheeks.

"Why are you bawling?" Mitchell asked.

Aero told him then...just poured the whole thing out.

"Well, hell, man," Mitchell said, "why did you bury her? How stupid can you get? Get your ass back out there and dig her up."

"Dig her up? I can't do that!"

"Yes, you can. Dig her up and clean her up. Set her in a lawn chair and hose her down, or if she's too stiff, lay her down on the patio and hose her until there's not a speck of dirt on her. Pay attention to her hair and every crease and crevice. Be sure there's no dirt in her nose or ears."

"Mitchell, I just can't do that."

The restroom door opened and a man came in. He said nothing. Walked into a stall without acknowledging Aero and Mitchell. For a long moment Mitchell remained quiet, then changed the subject. "We could go see the wresting match when I get back."

"Yes," Aero said.

"That'll be a week from next Thursday," Mitchell said. Shortly thereafter the stranger left the stall and walked out the door without troubling to come near them to wash his hands.

"Her hair was always set. I can't do that," Aero said. "I just can't dig her up anyway."

"You damn well better or you'll have a lot bigger problem. Listen to me. Be sure you have her really clean, dry her off real good and put clothes on her ... maybe just a nightgown, then put her back by the fireplace where she fell. Maybe place something she could have fallen over. She'll be found. It'll look like she just had an accident and with her bad heart, you'll be home free. You don't know anything about it, see?"

"I stand to inherit her...house and whatever she has," Aero said.

"All the more reason to look innocent. Damn it, Aero stop bawling. Get out of here and get digging as soon as it's dark."

"I can't. Besides, I have to work."

"I'll tell Hector you ate something that made you sick. Get going and do just exactly as I said."

"I just can't do it. It would dig up her roses."

Mitchell punched Aero in his shoulder. "If you don't do it, you can just forget our ever getting together again. And the big, wonderful surprise I have for you could vanish into thin air."

Aero shook his head. "I guess I just have to try. I never meant to hurt her."

"I know. It was an accident," Mitchell said. "You just have to make it look like a slightly different accident. I think Helen would want you to do it this way."

Aero brightened. "You think so? Yes, she probably would. She was so protective of me."

"Out the door and gone," Mitchell said giving him a pat on his back.

Aero looked at Mitchell briefly, then turned to leave.

"Very, very clean," Mitchell reminded him.

***

On the way over to Helen's, Aero spoke aloud to himself. "I'm not gonna hose her down. No, I ain't gonna do that. It would mess up her hair set. Besides, I wrapped her up pretty good in that sheet and blanket. No, it was that yellow flowered comforter, I think." In his preoccupation he ran slightly off the edge of the road, but recovered before he went into the ditch. It was then he noticed how badly he was trembling. Better calm down. Have to think. Yes, have to keep her hair set. So what if there's a little dirt. He could say she helped him set out the rose bushes. That would explain dirt except better not dress her in a gown. She'd have bathed before putting on a gown.

He pulled off the highway and drove up into her backyard. It was twilight now. He looked around but saw no one. Anyway, Helen's house was not close to a neighbor. Horace Jackson was closest, and that was about a quarter of a mile down the hill. Still, there was a path that ran back of the hill houses so he'd better wait until it was dark before digging.

While sitting in the car waiting for nightfall, he thought of her suitcase with clothes and her purse in it. He'd get all of them out, and he'd put the money back in the purse. If muddy water seeped into the suitcase, he couldn't leave things wet and dirty. He could put them in the washing machine. Helen never bought a piece of clothing she couldn't wash. Dry cleaning was such a waste of money, she'd said. "Why I could buy another dress for what it would cost to keep dry cleaning the thing." He could almost hear her speaking. Besides, she'd said, washed clothes smelled better. But if he washed the dresses, he'd have to dry them and maybe iron them. That could take hours and he wasn't much at ironing. He'd sure have to replant the roses, too.

At nightfall, he got out of the car and began digging. Fortunately, the ground was soft now and he hadn't buried her more than about three feet deep. He heard laughter and conversation. Someone was walking up the path. He slipped behind his car and waited. Three teenagers. Boys scuffling and catcalling. Would they go on past or did they plan to rob Helen...likely knowing she lived alone? So many gangs now. He slipped back in his car soundlessly leaving the door ajar...glad now his old car didn't light up inside, but the boys went on their way. He sighed in relief, quickly left his car and resumed digging. Now with concern about discovery, he worked as fast as he could. Digging, digging, digging and going down deeper in the soil. He felt the dampness seep in on his ankles and then on his pant legs. Sweat dripped from his face and he fought off mosquitoes. Three feet seemed deeper now in his rush.

When he saw the wrapped body, he suddenly felt sick. No, no time! He steeled himself against the surge in his stomach, reached down and grasped the comforter with both hands. She was not stiff. Although, limp she not heavy. He was able to pull her body up and out. After he placed her aside, he reached for the suitcase. Grab the handle and pull it out. Hurry up! Set the suitcase down, fill up the hole and reset the rose bushes. Fast! He broke into a sweat as he worked. In the distance he heard church chimes. It was time for Wednesday night prayer meeting.

He fished for the key to Helen's back door and let himself in with her body, then retrieved the suitcase and set it inside as well. No lights! Get the yard in proper shape. Hurry! Hurry! His body was wet with sweat and his nose itched and dripped, but the job was done. He replaced the shovel. Oh, no, wash it off with the hose. Helen always wanted it put up clean. He washed it, then hung the hose up neatly the way she liked it done.

Inside the house he turned on a lamp and unwrapped her body. Oh! Her face was gray, her mouth gaped, and her eyes were open in little slits. She was damp and her gown was soaked but her hair set still looked pretty good. He searched around in her closet and her chest of drawers for a shirt and slacks. Underwear? Yes, better do that, too. Shoes? Bedroom slippers? No. Oxfords.

Once she was dressed, he placed her as Mitchell had suggested. Maybe it would work. He unpacked the suitcase and cleaned off the dirt before putting it back in the bottom of the closet. He put the bloody sheets and the comforter in the washing machine, and poured in a generous amount of detergent. Helen had once said to wash blood in cold water. He punched on *cold* and *extra large*. The water began pouring in. Oh, her purse! He opened it, replaced the money, and set the purse on a side table where she usually kept it.

For a long moment he stood to survey the scene. Had he forgotten anything? He didn't think so. Oh, but his fingerprints on the bag and on her purse! He carefully wiped both as best he could. His fingerprints elsewhere probably wouldn't matter.

At the door he looked back. Tears came now. "Goodnight, Helen," he said. He closed and locked the door. On second thought, he unlocked the door, wiped the knob, locked again and wiped the outside knob as well. He glanced around but saw no one. The moon was up and lit the rose bushes like twilight. Had anyone seen his car? Would that matter? He got in and drove off back down the hill toward his apartment.

***

April worried. What could she do about Mitchell showing up again...especially at the hospital after the baby was born? Should she have a restraining order put on him? How could she do that without giving a reason? She didn't think she could. She needed to talk with someone, but who? She thought of Aero. Would he have any influence on Mitchell? She sighed heavily.

From what she'd seen, it didn't appear to be a two-way friendship, more like boss and servant. No, that one was out.

She could tell Mama and get sympathy, but also add to her mother's worries. Dad would be ready to beat up Mitchell. That wouldn't do. Mary Jean would, like Mama, be sympathetic, and she'd try her best to protect her. But she really couldn't help significantly, and it didn't seem a fair thing to do anyway. April dropped her head in her hands. She felt truly alone. At first she didn't hear the doorbell. Was that Mitchell again? Would he keep bothering her endlessly? She rushed to peer out the little side window. No, it was Kelly.

She opened the door and invited him in.

He smiled, but then frowned. "Did I come at a wrong time?"

"No. I...I was just trying to figure out a problem."

"Anything I can do?"

"No. What do you want?"

"To see how you are feeling, and if you have any information to pass on to me," he said.

"I'm all right, but no, I have no information to pass on. Not of any significance. Dell tried to convince me to set a deadline for the murder to be solved. He's convinced it won't be solved and he wants money now. I wouldn't give in, but he's having some timber cut on the old home place so he'll have a little cash. Hope he doesn't go to the casino."

"Don't let that worry you. You look pale and sad. Has someone upset you? You don't need that now with your baby due soon." His voice was so kind it touched her. She fought tears.

"You know they say pregnant women become emotional," she said and turned aside so he couldn't see the tears that betrayed her.

He reached to embrace her but didn't. Instead he said, "Whatever bothers you, you can tell me. I only want to help you."

She wiped her tears on the back of her hands. "Thank you," she said.

"Let me help," he said.

The tears came again and this time he embraced her. "Tell me what is hurting you," he said. "I care about you."

Should she tell him? It occurred to her in that moment, she might avoid Mitchell if she went to a hospital away from Columbus. She lingered in Kelly's embrace feeling comforted. "Could you possibly take me to a hospital out of town when my baby is due? I know it's a lot to ask, but I want it to be private."

"Where do you want to go?" he asked.

"Aberdeen, I think. My doctor lives in a big, country house on a farm about half way between Columbus and Aberdeen. He practices at both places so it won't be a problem for him."

"Why do you want to do that? Are you trying to avoid someone?" He asked.

"Yes," she said. She moved away and sat on a nearby sofa. He joined her there and took her hand in his hand.

"Who is bothering you?" he asked.

"You don't know him," she said.

"The captain you were dating?"

Her heart raced. Had he guessed? He may have known all along, more than she realized. "Yes," she said. "He's been coming around and I don't want to see him. He says he's getting a divorce so we can be married. I don't want that."

"Would you like to put a restraining order on him?"

"No. I just want to avoid him," she said.

"You don't want him to visit you at the hospital?"

"No, and he's said he would."

"Call me when the first pains start and I'll take you. Day or night. He removed a small notebook from his shirt pocket and wrote down a telephone number. "My cell phone," he explained and handed it to her.

"Can you do that without telling anyone? I really don't want anyone at all outside my family to know."

"Yes, I can." He pulled her close and kissed her forehead. "I'll take care of you," he said. "When should I expect the call?"

"Due date is August fifteenth, but I'm told babies come when they get ready." She smiled. The relief she felt was more wonderful than she'd imagined it could be.

"I have to go now, but I'll be thinking of you," he said.

She walked with him to the door. She touched his arm and faced him. "Thank you so much," she said.

"I think I love you," he said.

She smiled. "Oh," she said softly.

He took her in his arms and kissed her and she responded warmly. It could be easy to love him, but was it too soon? After her initial feelings of exasperation and resentment toward him, she'd begun to feel comfortable in their meetings. Always she'd considered him handsome.

"You're wonderful," she said, "I feel so much better now."

"Call me if you need anything," he said, and walked out the door. She watched him go. He turned briefly to look at her once again, smiled, then made his way down the steps.

***

Faith Ann drove up to the old mansion at exactly ten o'clock. Dell came down the steps. He was dressed in a tan and white pinstripe suit, white shirt and tan tie matching the pinstripe. His black hair, thinning on top, was neatly combed back over his ears and tied in a short ponytail.

"You look very nice," Faith Ann said.

"Thanks," he said. He smiled revealing small almost baby-like teeth. "Where's your mother?" he asked as he looked around before entering the car.

"She didn't feel up to going. Mother has a number of health problems. Has good days and bad days."

Dell opened the car door and got in. "Hey," he said, "you look good yourself, but then you always do." His best feature, his typical Stembridge round, blue eyes crinkled when he smiled.

"Thanks," she said. "This blue dress is old and a bit faded, but I like it. Mother said it's getting shabby, and if I don't stop wearing it she's going to put it in the rag bag." She smiled and flipped her long black hair from her neck. It did little good, the curls fell back into place.

"Your dress and all of you look good to me," Dell said.

"Thanks."

Before she drove off, she frowned. "Your house needs painting. Buy some paint and I'll help you paint it when I have free time."

"You're a house painter?" he asked, as she put the car in gear.

"I'm not helpless," she said and laughed. "Before my dad died, he taught me to do lots of stuff. I can paint with the best of them, build cabinets and do minor electrical work. Which reminds me, what do you do, Dell? Your job, I mean."

"I don't have a job right now," he said. "I've been into gaming."

"Gaming? Isn't that gambling?" she said driving and keeping her eyes on the road now.

"Well, yeah," he said, "but I'm about to have some timber cut."

"Pine? Pulpwood?"

"Yes. I have two cutters to call. One who chooses tree by tree and saves the seed trees and one who clean cuts."

"I imagine you'll choose the one who saves the seed trees. We need to think of the future, whether we actually get there or not."

"Yeah," Dell mumbled. Always into instant gratification, he thought *no way, baby, that's less money.*

She glanced at him. "Are you concerned about the future?" she asked.

"Not really," he said.

"Are you sure? With such tragedy in the world, war and all, I do wonder what's next. Does your minister think we're moving toward Armageddon?"

He frowned. "What do you think?"

"Don't know, of course, but there're signs, don't you think? Does your minister make any mention of it?"

"Not that I know of," Dell said. He stirred uncomfortably in his seat. "Are we getting close to the church now?"

"About five more miles," she said. "What church do you attend?"

"I haven't been in a while," he said. "I used to go with my grandfather."

"Is he still living?"

"No."

"I suppose you miss him," she said. "I sure miss my dad."

"I miss him in more ways than one," Dell said.

"What about your dad?"

"Gone. Both my parents are deceased."

"Any brothers and sisters?" she asked and added, "I had a sister but she died soon after birth. I've always wished she could have lived."

"Sorry, no, I was an only child," Dell said. "I had older first cousins, but they're dead, too. You may have known about them. They owned the antique store."

"Yes, I read about it. Neither the murder nor the shooting has been solved yet, has it? So sad," she said, "I'm sorry."

"I don't think it ever will be solved," he said.

"Why? Sometimes it takes a long time, but it may still happen."

"Scotland Yard ain't on the case," he said.

She glanced at him. "You sound bitter. It must be disappointing to you."

"Nothing I can do about it," he said.

She slowed down and turned off the pavement onto a gravel road. "The church is just around this curve," she said. "These are really nice people. We lived out here until Daddy died, and then we moved into town so I could get a job."

The church was an old fashioned white structure with a steeple, but a ramp for the handicap had been built to the side of the steps. When Faith Ann drove up, a small group had gathered out front. A young girl pushed a thin, white-haired man in a wheelchair, up the ramp.

"That's Dr. Smithfield in the wheelchair. Such a kind, gentle man. He made house calls...practically unheard of today. That's his granddaughter taking care of him." She glanced at Dell. "Family is so important. I hope to have children one day. Oh, not just to take care of me when I'm old." She laughed. "I love the little crumb crunchers."

"Yeah," he mumbled. He remembered she'd helped out in Vacation Bible School but chose to let that thought go. He opened the car door. Kids and old age weren't anything he wanted to think about. He closed his door and went around to open hers, but Faith Ann was already out and reaching for a picnic hamper on the back floorboard.

A large, older woman rushed up to embrace her. "Oh, Faith Ann, I'm so glad to see you, child. Where's your Mama?"

Faith Ann returned her embrace. "Great to see you, too, Mrs. Haulton. Mother didn't feel too well. Oh, this is Dell Stembridge, Mrs. Haulton."

"Howdy, young man," the smiling woman said, "and welcome." She extended a brown, wrinkled hand to shake hands.

Dell took her hand and bowed slightly. "Thanks, ma'am."

Faith Ann reached again take out the picnic hamper.

"Honey, let the young man do that," Mrs. Haulton said. "Men lift the heavy things."

Dell flushed. "Yes, I'll get it," he said.

***

Inside the church, two large, square fans up front hummed as they stirred the air. The plain church windows were closed on one side of the small sanctuary, but open on the other, where a grove of large oak trees offered shade and cooler air. On a platform up front on one side was a piano. A thin lady with freckled arms and graying red hair played a medley of hyms while the congregation assembled. From time to time, she peered over her horn-rimmed glasses to look at the crowd.

The program sheet on plain, white paper announced the topic of the sermon as "What Causes Hate?" Four songs were listed...old familiar church songs that Dell remembered hearing his grandfather, in his tenor voice, belt out above other voices in the congregation. His grandmother often whispered, "Sean, don't sing so loud." It did no good, and as a kid he'd felt embarrassed.

The minister, a portly gentleman with gray temples and a serious face began with the scripture. "Turn your Bibles to John, Chapter 16, verses 2 and 3." He waited while some members of the congregation opened their Bibles and turned pages, before he read the scripture. "...the time cometh when whosoever killeth you will think that he doeth God service. And these things they will do unto you, because they have not known the Father, nor me."

The minister paused before he spoke. "Is this not what is happening now? Does this not speak of our need for missions? Our God is love...not hate...not a murderer. I hope each of you will do your part in spreading knowledge of Jesus and our father God, all over the world. The collections today will be especially for these missions."

Dell barely heard the rest of the sermon. So they wanted money. He felt uncomfortably warm and out of place. He longed for the sermon and the singing to be over so he could eat the good food and leave. If only he had money to go to the casino tonight! Missing the bright lights, the fun and excitement felt like such deprivation. As soon as he got home, he'd call Jubal Boy and get the timber clear cut and the money ... the glorious money, as soon and as much as possible! He glanced at Faith Ann. Somehow now she had faded in his estimation...just a pretty little country girl taken up by religion. He might, however, get her to do some free work on his house.

Chapter Fourteen

Now that he had riches, Marvelous was a proud man. He stopped working immediately after returning home from Europe, bought a Lexus and drove around dressed in expensive sports clothes. His wildest dreams had come true now that women, who had ignored him in the past, were eager to have his attention. He frequented nightclubs and the best restaurants. He left town and made no attempt to hide his female companions.

At Hector's, Marvelous spent money wildly, often treating the crowd to drinks and food. Showy, outrageous tips brought him instant service from the staff. Flirtatious women snuggled up to him, and kissed him when he stuffed bills into the cleavage of their low cut blouses. Then Casey, a voluptuous redhead, who had an endless list of things she wanted him to buy for "little ole" her, became his nightly companion.

At first Flaudie Mae suffered in private, but she finally told a friend who, in turn, told April. April was awakened in late morning with the news. Although it was August fifteenth, the due date for the birth of her baby, April got in her car and drove to Watsonville. On her drive she thought she should have had Jayson drive her, but she was feeling no symptoms, so she trusted she would be all right. Anyway, she'd heard first babies often take longer to arrive, even after the contractions begin.

Once inside her parents home, April found her mother and embraced her. "Mama, why didn't you tell me?"

"I didn't want to worry you, honey. Just forget it. There's nothing I can do about it."

"Yes, there is. You can tell him you're both going to marriage counseling, and if that doesn't work, you can get a divorce."

"He won't go. You know how he is," Flaudie Mae said.

"His bank account is going to dry up if he doesn't," April said. "I should never have given him such a large amount of money in the beginning."

"It's not your fault."

"In a way, it is," April said. "I'm going to tell him what the rules are."

But Marvelous was not home. It soon became clear he'd skipped town with the red haired Casey.

"He'll be back when the money runs out," April said. "In the meantime, Mama, pack your clothes and come stay with me in Columbus."

"He'll be mad if I'm gone when he returns," Flaudie Mae said.

"Mama! So what? Pack your clothes. Here, let me help you," April said. She went to a closet, took out a bag and began packing clothes.

April heard a car draw up outside. She glanced out the window and saw her father.

A few minutes later Marvelous came into the room. "What are you doing?" he asked.

"Mama is going home with me. Listen up, Dad, you're not getting another dime from me until you stop your foolishness."

"What foolishness?"

"One example I think is Casey."

"Oh, she's just a friend."

"Not a dime more, and you and Mama are going into counseling."

"Don't tell me what to do!"

"All right. When you spend what you have, you're out of money. Get a job."

"April," he said. His voice trembled. "Baby, I have...I'm sick."

"What?"

"I went to the doctor. Had something wrong."
"What?" She frowned. He'd always fought going to doctors.
"A drainage." He flushed. "I caught somethin' bad."
"What?" April asked.
"Somethin' like 'gone-to-rear'"
"Gonorrhea," April said.
"Yeah," he said, "Musta been bugs on them toilets in Europe."
April shook her head. Flaudie Mae's eyes filled with tears. Marvelous continued in a quaking voice, "The doc said I have HIVS, too...AIDS. I've got AIDS." He broke into sobs. "I'm gonna die."
Flaudie Mae rushed to embrace him.
"I'm sorry, I'm sorry," he cried gathering her close to himself.
April went to him then and joined in the embrace. "We'll get the best possible treatment for you Daddy," she said.

***

Back at home in Columbus, April felt tired. She went to her bedroom to lie down, but as soon as she entered the room, the telephone rang. She slipped in the chair beside her bed and caught her breath before she answered.
"April, are you all right? How are you feeling?" Kelly asked.
"Oh, John, I've just had such bad news. My father has been careless and now he has AIDS. I'm afraid I'm partly responsible."
"Now how could that be your fault?"
"I should have known he couldn't handle a large amount of money. He became reckless with it and had contact with...with somebody he shouldn't have."
"I'm sorry, honey," he said, "but it's not your fault."

"I know he's not been a very good husband and father, but Mama and I love him anyway. I'm going to help him all I can, but, John, he's going to die. I know it's a fatal disease."

"Yes, and that's hard news for you and for your mother," he said, " but with treatment he may live quite a while, even longer than you expect."

"Mama is completely loyal to him no matter what, and Dad's not easy to care for when he's sick. He gets alarmed even when he has minor illnesses...he's so sure he's going to die with even a small case of the sniffles. He's really going to suffer now and Mama will have to keep trying to comfort him."

"The timing is bad, too. You didn't say how you are feeling. This is the day, isn't it?" he asked. "Actually, that was the main reason I called."

"It was supposedly the day, but I don't feel anything except tired. I'll call if anything happens, and thank you, John, for checking on me."

"Don't forget I'm going to look after you. That's a promise. Now get some rest and call me, if and when you need me."

"I will."

When they said their goodbyes, she hung up the receiver, kicked off her sandals and lay down on the bed. Within minutes she was asleep.

***

As expected, Helen's body was found when she didn't show up for work. Ginny, a co-worker, went to her home. When Helen didn't answer the door Ginny peeked through a crack in the Venetian blinds and saw Helen lying on the hearth. She immediately called the police with her cell phone and waited until they arrived.

The police checked the house. A robbery did not appear involved as nothing seemed missing from her home. The coroner made only a sketchy examination considering that her medical information revealed a serious heart problem. Aero was questioned, but Mitchell claimed the two of them were together at the time of her death. The alibi plus Aero's flood of tears convinced the authorities he was innocent of her murder and was indeed grief stricken over her death.

Aero planned her funeral and arranged for a marble headstone to later be put in place. It was to read "Helen Madison, born June 2, 1975, died August 12, 2004. A good woman. The last little leaf on her family tree." Since he lacked the funds to pay for the funeral and the headstone, he had to convince the mortuary to wait until he could collect the inheritance. After he signed the proper notarized papers, he was allowed the arrangement.

When they left the cemetery, Mitchell said, "You see I was right about digging her up. Now you can move from your apartment to her house and have a little cash left over."

"I'll first have to pay off the loan against the house. She didn't have that much cash money, and her old car won't bring much."

"Yes, Aero, but what if you'd left her buried? You need to listen to me. Now keep your mouth shut. Don't go around blabbing and bawling, and quit hitting the bottle. Who knows what you could let slip."

"I don't drink at Hector's anymore. I just drink at home."

"Stay off the damn drugs and quit chipping and carving on yourself. You act like a fool," Mitchell said. "First thing you know you'll be back in the mental hospital and you could say too much there. Big time. Too much!"

"I'm not unconscious when I'm there."

"Maybe not, but the doc might pick it out of you." Mitchell sighed heavily. "Just do the hell what I say. No booze and no drugs."

Aero said, "You could show me a little appreciation. A little love now and then."

"Appreciation, you've got. Love, that's something else," Mitchell said.

They walked on in silence then until they reached Mitchell's car.

"I want you to check on April," Mitchell said. "See if she'll talk to you. She's turned me off."

***

As was customary when he could arrange it, Mitchell telephoned home and talked with his wife every Thursday night.

Five-year-old Warren answered the telephone. "Daddy! Daddy!" he cried. "when you coming home?"

"Can't come right away, son, but by Thanksgiving anyway. How are you? You liking kindergarten?"

"Yes. I like coloring in my airplane book. Mommy said the one on the front page is like the one you fly."

"Great. How is Sarah?"

"She had her birthday party today. That why you called?"

"Yes and no. I wanted to talk with you, and Sarah and your mother."

"I'll get Sarah," Warren said. "Did you know she's four now?"

Mitchell laughed. "Yes, I reckon I knew that."

"Sarah!" Warren called. "Sarah, it's Daddy!"

Mitchell held the phone and waited.

"Daddy?" Sarah asked. "That you?"

"Yes, sweetheart. Happy birthday! How was your party?"

"I got lots of presents, and we had ice cream. We wore funny hats and ate cake. Mommy played the guitar, and we sang and sang. It was fun!"

"I'm glad."

"Mommy said wait a minute. She's feeding our kitten. We got a new one. He's black and white, and we named him Splash."

"Splash?"

"Yes, his white looks like it was white paint splashed on his back." She giggled.

Mitchell heard Marlene's voice. "Let mommy talk now. OK?"

"All right. Daddy, I got to put you up now. Mommy wants to talk to you."

"Hello, Mitch," Marlene said. "We had quite a party. Wish you could have been here."

"I will be there for her next one. Just eight more months of the Air Force, you know."

"I'll be so glad! I miss you."

"I miss you, too, honey. You know we have big plans for the future. I trust you're keeping everything going well."

"Oh, Mitch, I think you worry too much about our family being perfect," she said.

"Marlene, you know when I go into politics, they'll be looking at everything. I mean to run for Mayor of Lewisburg first, and they'll be checking us out in Beckly."

"I know only too well about your ambitions; politics up the ladder to fame and that house in Lewisburg, but don't reach too far. Up the ladder in politics I think you probably can manage, but the house in Lewisburg may not be for sale." She laughed.

He didn't laugh. "With enough money, it will be."

"You're not making sense," she said. "We don't have that kind of money."

He hesitated, then said, "We may have something to work through, but I think we'll eventually have the money."

"What do you mean?"

"Just forget that. What I want you to remember is that when we married the love was there, and that hasn't changed. It never will, no matter what."

"Have you been drinking? I don't understand what you're talking about," she said.

"No, I'm not drinking. It's just that I want you to understand even if we should have problems of any kind, we'll work through them. You're mine and that's what counts. Remember my goal is to eventually make you First Lady of West Virginia."

"Problems?" she asked. "What problems?"

"Oh, honey, all couples have problems now and then, but I just want us to be so committed so absolutely, so totally committed, that nothing breaks us apart and nothing makes us look bad to the public."

"I think you better tell me what problem you have in mind," she said. Her voice was firm.

"Now don't get upset. There's a girl down here who tried to get me to leave you and marry her. I'm definitely not going to do that, but if you hear about her when I'm running for office, I want you to know it means nothing. It was a little flirtation because I was lonesome, and I'm sorry as I can be about that, but she means nothing. It's over."

"Damn you, Mitch, you had an affair! I should kick your butt out. I've been true to you when, believe me, I didn't have to. I've had my chances, but I didn't take them. I've kept faithful to you and to our damned shining reputation." She slammed the phone down and refused to answer it when he called back.

***

Mitchell walked away from the telephone, left the officer's barracks and got in his car. "Well," he said to himself, "I laid the groundwork. That was tough, but what could I do? Just show up with the baby and say, 'Hey, honey, look what I brought home for us?' Had to do it. Well, she'll get over it."

He drove to a flower shop, walked in and ordered two dozen red roses to be sent to Marlene. He wrote a note. "Like I said, you're my dearest one, Mitch."

He got back in his car and drove to April's home. He parked and walked up to the porch to ring the doorbell. The floodlights were on all around the mansion, something he strongly disliked. He'd hoped to have April open the door and then see him. As it was, anyone could see him. He rang the doorbell again and Mary Jean appeared.

"I'd like to see Mrs. Stembridge," Mitchell said. "Just for a short time."

"I'm sorry sir, but she has already gone to bed. I'll tell her you came by."

"That's all right. No need to disturb her." He turned to go, but turned back as if having an after thought "Has her baby come yet?"

"No, Sir."

He walked back to his car. The birth should be any day now. He'd keep checking.

***

Faith Ann arrived at Dell's doorstep at eight o'clock sharp on Monday morning. The bell didn't work, but she banged on the door until the sleepy-eyed Dell showed up.

"Why are you here at dawn?" he asked.

"Dawn was four hours ago, Dell Stembridge. Get out of them pajamas into your clothes. We have the whole day to work," she said.

He sighed heavily. "You can start. I'll get up a little later."

"No, you get dressed. I brought you a box breakfast," she said and handed the box to him.

"Well, thanks," he said, taking the food and turning back in the hallway.

"Eat up and join me," she said. "Looks like cleaning this place comes first. I'll fix the doorbell. Probably just needs a little re-wiring."

Dell made his way to his kitchen, shoved back a stack of dirty dishes and prepared to eat from the box. Inside he saw scrambled eggs, sausage, toast, orange juice and coffee. Good deal! He ate hungrily. Before he finished the last bite, he heard the doorbell. Gosh, the first time in probably five years at least. That girl was something else!

Faith Ann came into the kitchen. "Good heavens!" she said. "When's the last time you washed dishes?"

"Dishwasher don't work," he said.

She opened it and looked inside. "Get me a screw driver," she said.

"If I can find one." He scratched around in a kitchen drawer, closed it and tried another one. "Here we are," he said. He handed her the tool.

"Get your work clothes on," she said.

He left while she worked on the dishwasher. He heard her singing something about "Let me walk with Thee." A Christian song he'd heard long ago but had all but forgotten.

When he returned Faith Ann handed him a note. "Go to the hardware store and buy these parts. I've written the details down."

"Can't," he said. "I don't have the money."

"You can't charge it?"

"No. I don't think so."

"Well, the repair will have to wait until you do have the money. In the meantime, we'll hand wash this mess." She removed the dishes and pans from the double sink, poured in some cleanser and scrubbed. "At least you have dishwashing products." She laughed. "Of course you do, you haven't used any in who knows when."

She filled the first sink with some dried on dirty dishes and ran hot water and dishwashing liquid over them. "We'll let them soak a bit while we do the floors. Where's your vacuum cleaner?"

"I think it's in a closet. I'll check," he said.

She followed him and found he was right. She took a look. "Dell," she said, "this vacuum cleaner needs a clean bag. Where are they?"

"Maybe in the top of the closet." He searched but didn't find any there.

Faith Ann sighed. "Well, we'll have to have some. I'll add them to the list."

"I told you I don't have any money."

"When is your timber being cut?"

"Day after tomorrow."

"Very well. We'll clean up the kitchen today and I'll leave. In the meantime if you get your timber money, buy the list of things, including anything else I find we'll need, to get this place in shape."

"I'll let you know," Dell said, but knew he wouldn't. Soon as he got that money, he'd be off to the casinos.

Like she could read his mind, she said, "Don't you gamble that new money away. You might like to eat in the future."

"I got some inheritance money coming later," he said. "If you'd lend me the money, I'd go get the stuff now."

"No loan, Dell. Look, I'm willing to give you my free labor and know-how, but not if you're going to gamble," she said.

"You're tough," he said.

"How do you think I've survived with nobody to help me? I'm proud I'm tough, but I like you. I want you to behave smarter, that's all."

After three hours all the dishes, pans and utensils were clean and put away. The kitchen windows sparkled and the ceramic tile floor was clean. Underneath all the clutter, three cans of soup and a jar of strawberry jam showed up. No other food except peanut butter was in evidence in the cabinets or in the now clean, baking soda-scented refrigerator.

"Here," Faith Ann said. She reached in her pocket and withdrew five dollars. "This is not a loan. It's a gift. Maybe the only one you'll ever get from me, but go buy yourself a box of dry milk and a loaf of bread. I see you have peanut butter."

"Thanks," he said.

"I'm sorta paying you for all the hard work you did in the kitchen. I noticed your grunts and groans," she said and laughed.

"Dry milk?" He wrinkled his nose.

"Yes, you'll find it in a box at the supermarket. Directions for mixing it with water are on the box. Makes good milk, especially chilled overnight in the refrigerator."

"I'll pay you back when I get my timber money," he said.

"If you wish, but you don't have to. Try to clean at least one of the bathrooms before I return, but I'm gone now."

How could that starchy person be in the body of a pretty, young girl? She seemed more like a mother. Not like his own, but like his friend, Sam Smith's mother. Sam, who became a doctor, and left Columbus for the university hospital in Birmingham. But heck, he didn't need all that study and work. He just needed some luck at the casinos.

When they walked down the hallway to the front door, she said, "You might consider renting a room in this big house. A college boy may need a room and kitchen privileges. It would give you some income. Of course, choose a serious student, not some party boy."

Dell frowned. "I don't know about that. I have some pretty valuable stuff in my house."

"You could check references and know the reputation of the boy. Maybe even one from your church."

"Yeah," he mumbled. "Maybe."

When they walked out the front door, she said, "Dell, look at your lawn. It needs work. Come with me and let me show you what you need to do first."

Reluctantly, he followed her outside where she described trimming and shaping some of the shrubs.

He grunted acceptance. "When I can get to it," he said.

At her car door, she moved close to him and looked up. "Bye," she said. Her voice soft, almost a whisper.

He thought there was a message in it, like *kiss me*. He took a chance and found her response exciting. Now he was confused. Where did this sweetheart come from, and the mother in her go?

She gently removed herself from his embrace, opened the door to her old, bright blue Chevrolet and got in. "Bye," she said again, started the engine, and drove off.

Chapter Fifteen

Chief Hillman closed the door to his office, proceeded to his desk and took his seat. He spoke to Kelly and deputies Carter and Henry. "Let's see where we are at this point in the Stembridge case," he said. "John have you something to report?"

"Yes, sir," Kelly said. "The captain, Mitchell Redmond, is pressuring April to marry him when he gets a divorce. Funny thing, though, I checked with Clemson, my counterpart in Redmond's hometown, and learned no divorce is in progress, and Clemson thinks none will be. He says the Redmonds appear to be close knit...an ideal young family. He believes the captain, whom he's known since high school, is more than capable of affairs, but doubts he'd leave Marlene."

"What do you make of that?" Hillman asked.

"I think he's interested in April's baby which he believes is his. Just how he thinks that will benefit him without April, is the question. I'm afraid...I'm thinking April may be in danger after the baby is born."

"How do you figure that?" Hillman asked.

Kelly said, "I believe you know, Chief. Probably thought of it long before now. If April were out of the way and if the baby is his, a fortune in inheritance is involved."

"Right, but do you think he'd murder her?" Hillman asked.

"Not so anyone could call it that. I think he'd try to make her death look like an accident, but I don't know. Of course, this is all speculation."

Hillman pressed his fingertips together. "In any event, she appears to have a problem. We need to keep watch on her," he said, "and we'll keep a tap on her phone."

Kelly said, "She has a security system at home and I don't believe she'd let him in the house. When she's outside her home may be when she's most vulnerable. I'll set up protection for her."

"I trust she has a battery back-up to her security system in case the electricity is cut," Carter said.

"She does, and she has a cell phone in case her land line is cut," Kelly said.

"So we put a watch on the captain. How do you figure this relates to the murder and attempted murder of her husband and sister-in-law? Henry asked.

"I don't know if there is a relationship. We have a list of suspects who could have done that for their own reasons. For instance, like Juke Box. He could have done it just out of revenge for not being given the amount of money he wanted, and the fact he seems to have contempt for rich people."

The Chief said, "It could have been one of the other suspects, but I still get back to the fact that all of the Stembridge problems occurred after April entered their lives.".

Kelly frowned. "Yes, Chief, but I don't think she personally did anything to hurt them."

"I see you have feelings for her, John. Don't get in too deep. This crime is still in the guessing game. I will say, however, like you, I don't think she did anything intentionally to hurt them, and that she possibly could now be in real danger herself."

"I agree," Kelly said.

Hillman then turned to the deputies. "What have you observed of the captain and his side kick at the wrestling matches?"

Henry spoke first. "That the big guy seems dumb."

"Aero, you mean?" Hillman asked.

"Yes, sir. He acts like Redmond's servant. Jumps to serve him...gets him food or drink which Aero appears to always pay for."

Carter said, "Exactly, but I think he does it because he wants to. He seems so eager to please Redmond."

Kelly said, "The man is bisexual and has a big crush on Redmond."

Hillman asked, "What do you think? What do each of you think? Would Aero murder to please Redmond?"

None of the men answered immediately. Kelly was first to speak. "I think he might do anything short of that, but murder for him? I don't know."

Carter said, "He might. He's pretty much a puppy dog. I think Aero is a fool, but maybe not a total fool."

Henry said, "I'm more in agreement with John. If Redmond wants April out of the way, he'd try to arrange an accident, and maybe that would in some way involve Aero."

The chief said, "Whether or not this is a two-part matter with someone like Juke Box or Dell doing the other crime, we need to set up a watch for April. I think she could be in danger." He rose from his chair. "That's all for now. Good work. We'll meet again next week, or before if we have reason to do so."

John sighed. He'd kept his promise not to mention driving April to Aberdeen when the birth pains started, but did Hillman really need to know that?

***

Once in his car, Kelly dialed April's number on his cell phone. Mary Jean answered.

"This is Detective Kelly. Is Mrs. Stembridge available?" he asked.

"No, sir. She's gone to Watsonville to see her parents. She said for me to tell you if you called."

"Did she drive herself?" Kelly asked.

"No, Jayson drove her, but she said she felt all right. She's worried 'bout her parents."

"Do you know when she'll be back?"

"She said not until after supper. She likes to eat her mama's cooking."

"I see. Well, that still might be before eight o'clock with daylight savings now. I'll call her later. Thanks, Mary Jean."

"You're welcome, sir."

Kelly sat for a moment thinking about his next move. It occurred to him he should find out how much Juke Box observed of that football game the night of the murder. If he took time out, he'd have missed some major plays. Since he'd already committed himself to watching the game, that would allow discussion. Kelly smiled. He knew old man Dan Fina was a football fanatic who recorded many games. Maybe he had a recording of the game that night.

He drove down the street and turned right on Third street. In a small house set back from the street was Fina's house. Kelly parked his car and raced up to the door. Maybe, just maybe, he'd come up with a method of getting an unexpected clue on Juke Box.

Kelly felt in luck when Fina answered the door and said he was sure he had the recording. "Come on in," Fina said waving his thin arm forward. He led the way through a room so filled with boxes, bags and stacks of newspapers that the furniture could barely be seen. Kelly wondered how the old man could stand the clutter. Clearly, he was a major pack rat.

The walls of the second room were lined with shelves of videos. Fina ran fingers over a few and selected one. At least he was an organized pack rat when it came to football records. "Here, this is it," he said. "Now that was a game to remember. I don't mind lending it to you, John, but I sure do want it back."

"You know me, Mr. Fina. I'll bring it back just as soon as I finish watching the game."

"Enjoy! Enjoy!" Fina said.

Kelly waved and smiled. He drove to his apartment, turned on his television and pushed in the video.

He took a pad and pen in hand and started making notes while the game played. With his remote control he skipped the advertisements and the entertainment sections with music and cheers. He tried to keep focused on his mission, but at times he indulged himself. When the game reached high pitch excitement, he became involved and watched for pleasure, but he re-wound each time as necessary. Finally, he finished, turned off the television and prepared to visit Juke Box.

On his drive over, he passed a Colonel Sanders. What the heck, he'd turn around and take Juke Box at least a two-piece box of chicken with mashed potatoes and a biscuit. Maybe the food would throw him off guard and he'd say more than he meant to say. It was worth a couple of bucks to try anyway.

When he drove in the yard, Kelly saw Juke Box glance in his direction, but he resumed pulling a couple of tomatoes off a vine at the side of his trailer. At least the bum had grown himself a bit of food. Juke Box watched as Kelly left his car carrying the Colonel Sanders box.

"Did you get Original Recipe?" Juke Box asked.

"Sure did. Two pieces, mashed potatoes and a biscuit."

"Is that all? Man, why didn't you bring me a bucket? That's the way you people with money are. Cheap, cheap, cheap."

"I'm not so rich," Kelly said, "Guess that's how you felt when Mr. Stembridge didn't give you as much as you wanted."

"Right. Dern old rich bastard."

"What can you do about such people?" Kelly asked.

"Erase 'em. They ain't fit to live."

"Is that how you felt about Mr. Stembridge?"

"You bet your bonny browns!"

"Might as well just kill him, you think?"

"Yeah, I thought about it, but I didn't git the satisfaction. Somebody beat me to it."

"Do you know who?"

"Nope. Son-of-a-gun stole my satisfaction."

"Well, then did you try to make up for it by shooting Miss Stembridge?"

"Naw. Didn't think about that. I never ask broads for money, so I never get the urge to erase 'em like I would if they wuz cheap with me."

"Are you ever serious about anything?" Kelly said, "I think you joke about everything."

"Oh, I'm serious all right. Just has to fit my mood. Hey, drag up a chair and take the load off." He sat in the lawn chair by the table that still held a few black watermelon seeds. He yanked open the chicken box.

Kelly took the other rickety green lawn chair. "Let's talk a little football," Kelly said. "Am I right in thinking you have a good memory for the best and worst plays in a game?"

Juke Box didn't answer right away. He was gobbling the food. When he tossed a chicken bone aside he said, "I remember everything including which gal had the best legs."

"How about the game itself. What were the best plays you saw that night in November we talked about before...when 'Bama and Ole Miss played." Kelly said.

"I can do it and I will. Only big play I missed was the last one right at the end of the game. That was Roy's fault. He kept sitting there looking at me, wiggling his antenna. I knew he wanted something else to eat, so I gave in. When I was picking him a scrap out of the garbage I heard the crowd, but I was too late to see it. Damn Roy. I hate it when he does that to me."

"Tell me about the other plays," Kelly said.

"Man, why don't you watch the game for yourself. That's just like you people, wanting other people to nurse you through life."

"Indulge me," Kelly said. "After all, I brought you some Original Recipe."

To Kelly's amazement, Juke Box recited each significant play and named them in order. So much for his clever set up. April had found Clarence dead before that ballgame was over.

Kelly rose from his seat. "So long," he said.

"Next time bring me a bucket," Juke Box said.

Chapter Sixteen

April was glad she had asked Jayson to drive her. They had no sooner entered her car when she saw Mitchell drive slowly by. She knew, even at a glance, Mitchell could see Jayson was a big man. Still, she shivered. She felt she'd barely missed another unpleasant encounter.

When they were on their way, April said, "Jayson, from now on, for a while, I want you to drive me everywhere I go. I don't want to drive alone at least until after the baby is born."

"Yes, ma'am. Just let me know and I'll be there," Jayson said.

"I'll want you to go with me in the stores or wherever I go."

"Certainly. You don't need to be lifting and carrying things."

"Right," she said, but she knew she meant the post office as well, and how heavy were stamps?

How strange it was now to feel so uncomfortable in the presence of someone she'd been so crazy about only months before. Surely Mitchell wouldn't hurt her, but his demanding, controlling manner made her feel threatened. She continued to be deeply concerned about his insistence on being with her and the baby at the hospital and the demand for a DNA test. At least he would not know which hospital to visit. He would be thinking the Golden Triangle in Columbus, and he would be wrong.

When they reached her parents' home, April said, "Jayson, I think you wanted to go into town for some gasoline. Go ahead, but come back soon. Mama will have supper waiting for us."

"Yes ma'am," he said. "That will be a treat. I've heard what a great cook she is." He sprinted around the car and opened the door for April.

"See you later," she said, and walked toward the front door of her parents home.

Flaudie Mae met her at the door, hugged and kissed her. "I'm so glad you came, but honey should you be coming when you're past due?" She took April's hand and led her to the entry-way bench where they sat down.

"I don't feel anything but a little tired, Mama. It may be the doctor will have to induce labor."

"Could be, but maybe your count is off somehow. You probably remember Mrs. Dolly Creasen. I think her first baby came a whole month later than expected."

"I remember her, but I don't recall that," April said.

"Well, maybe you were too young to remember. Anyway, it's probably not too unusual to be early or late for different reasons. What does the doctor say?"

"He says everything looks normal, but 'we're apparently not quite ready,' like he's pregnant, too." April smiled. "He's very nice."

"Don't worry, then." Flaudie Mae hugged her again. "I made your peach cobbler," she said smiling.

"How is Daddy?" April asked. "On the phone this morning you said he's taking his medicines and watching a lot of television."

"Right now he's out with his hounds. He spends quite a lot of time with them. They give him lots of wet kisses and wait adoringly for anything he tells them to do. I'm glad he has them. It gives him more comfort than I can."

"I know he loves his dogs as if they were his sons," April said. She thought they're the *only* things he really loves. Earlier she'd resented that, but now she was glad he had them. She ran her hand over the mound of her stomach and wondered how he'd respond to his grandchild.

***

Dell watched as Jubal Boy worked his timber. The skidder knocked all the limbs off and cut the small trees into six-foot lengths for sawing. The squealing and clanking of the machinery and the pine scent filled the air. Dell smiled. Ah, the scent of money.

"What about the big trees?" Dell asked.

Jubal Boy spat out tobacco juice. "Them big'uns, we'll saw down. You got some good timber there," he said.

"How much money they gonna bring me?" Dell asked.

Jubal Boy stretched his skinny body and blinked his eyes. "Oh, can't exactly say. You know I gotta take it in and sell it. That's just the way it is. I'll send you a check."

"You must have some kind of notion. You been doing this a while," Dell said.

"Oh, probably...maybe four or five thou, but that's just a guess. Could be a bit more or less. Hey, I ain't gonna cheat you. It'll just be what it is, that's just the way it is."

"How soon will I get the money?"

"You in a hurry?"

"Yeah, I am."

"Well, I reckon I could bring your check by here in say three or four days. I got other rat killin' I gotta do."

"Three or four days! Couldn't I meet you somewhere before then?" Dell asked.

"Nope. That's it. That's just the way it is."

Dell snorted. "Well, if that's the best you can do, I suppose I have no choice."

"Nope. That's just the way it is."

"Don't say that again," Dell said and stomped back to his house.

Jubal Boy laughed. "Just the way it is," he shouted after Dell and resumed his work.

***

The days of waiting seemed unbelievably long to Dell. He stayed at home all day the third day but no Jubal Boy with a check.

The fourth day Faith Ann showed up. "I got today off. You have the money for us to buy the stuff we need?"

"Nope. Should be today. He said three or four days and this is the fourth day. No use you waiting around. Don't know when he'll get here or even if he will. People are not very dependable these days."

"I'll stay. We still have cleaning supplies and I betcha didn't clean even one of the bathrooms. Did you?"

Dell sighed. He wanted her to leave. If that check came he wanted to cash it and head for the casinos.

"You didn't answer me, so I know the answer," she said. "I know you hate to do cleaning, but Dell, it must be done."

"Why?" he asked. "Nobody here but me. Let's put it off. Come here and give me a goodbye kiss." He held out his arms for an embrace.

She laughed, but accepted his embrace and kiss.

"Wow," he said and kissed her again.

She moved aside. "That's enough for now."

"No, that's just a beginning," he said, pulling her back in for another kiss.

She again pulled away. "No more now. Maybe after we finish the cleaning."

Reluctantly, he joined her in cleaning the first bathroom. Before they could start on the second the doorbell rang.

"I'll get it," Dell said and raced to the front door. If that was Jubal Boy, he'd pocket the check and tell her something else. Maybe like somebody asking directions or a sales person.

It was Jubal Boy. The skinny timber man stood there waving a check in his hand. "You lucked up. Here's five thou and seventy-six dollars and two cents."

"Five thousand!" Faith Ann's voice startled Dell. He'd not heard her follow him down the hall.

"Yes, ma'am," Jubal Boy said. "You must be the lovely Mrs. Stembridge."

"No," Dell and Faith Ann said in unison.

Jubal Boy smiled. "Just don't have 'that little piece of paper'. I see. That's just the way it is lots of times these days."

"I'll take the check," Dell snapped. "Goodbye."

"Goodbye. Thanks for the job," Jubal Boy said, and made his way down the steps and back to his big logging truck parked on the street.

"Now," Faith Ann said, "we can go cash the check and deposit part of it. What do you think? It'll take about two thousand dollars for the paint, brushes and so forth alone. Fact is, might not be quite enough. We'll see. Then there're the other things. Parts for the dishwasher and Dell, you need to take your car in for inspection. You probably need an oil change and you need to fill it up with gas and have it washed. The lawn needs work. You probably should call the experts to deal with the lawn...it's pretty sad looking. Oh, and your beautiful Oriental rugs...well, that cleaning will probably have to wait. Anyway, you should have close two thousand to deposit in a bank account after expenses."

Dell's mind raced trying to think of a way to get rid of her. Her spending plan made sense and her kisses were sweet, but he yearned to hit the casinos.

"I don't think I feel up to it today," Dell said. "Maybe another time."

She said, "Like Elvis' song, 'It's Now or Never,' only in this case it's my *work* won't wait. If you're thinking of going to the casinos to blow that money, well, I'm just hanging it up, Dell."

"Ouch, do you mean that?"

"Yeah, I do. I'm trying to help you but if you want to play the fool, I'm gone." She turned to walk back through the house to get her purse.

"Don't go!" he cried.

"Are we going to be sensible or not?" she asked.

"Okay, you win. We'll do it your way," he said.

"Fine." She went to him, hugged and kissed him.

He held her close and kissed her again in a long kiss.

Breathlessly, she pulled away. "That's really exciting, Dell, but we have work to do."

"The work can wait," he said gathering her to himself again.

"No," she said.

"You're a tease," he said.

"I'm not. I feel just like you do, but I know what's right for us at this point."

It dawned on him then, as a Christian girl, she must be thinking of waiting until marriage. Marriage! He had no intention of getting married. He liked being free to do as he pleased, and he could see she would not allow that. Maybe it would be best to let her go now.

"I've changed my mind," he said. "I'm not going to do all that stuff you want me to do. I think we'd better just call the whole thing off."

She stared at him for a long moment. He saw her tears before she turned aside and resumed her plan to gather her purse.

"You and me just ain't a fit," he said.

"You're right," she said, now having regained her composure. She left then without looking back.

When she was gone, Dell spoke aloud to himself. "She was too damn practical. I did the right thing." He remembered his check, gave a little shout of joy, gathered up his car keys and left the house. He'd cash the check, fill the car up with gas and go!

***

Dell took the $5,000.00 he'd netted from the timber sale and drove to the casinos. His favorite had a western décor, where he felt most at home in blue jeans and cowboy boots. As a fellow gambler told him early in his career, "The next best thing to playing craps and winning is playing craps."

This time he counted on winning. He liked the $25.00 minimum bet tables, because they usually weeded out the lowlife losers who didn't know what they were doing and could screw up things for the gamblers who did. These were mostly the high rollers who made the game more fun.

He sidled in to the left of the next shooter, a distinguished looking older man who wore a white linen jacket and sported a moustache and goatee reminiscent of Col. Sanders. Dropping ten $100.00 bills onto the green felt, he smiled to the croupier and said, "Check change. All $25.00 chips." The dealer pushed four stacks of ten green chips over to him.

He placed two chips on the Pass Line--a $50.00 bet. The "Colonel" rolled a five. That was a decent point to make. Five pays three for two on bets, so he could back it with $100.00 and, if he made it, would win his $25.00 bet, plus $100.00 odds, and another $150.00. A total bet of $125.00 could net him a profit of $175.00

The elderly gent rolled a four, then an eight. On his third roll, he made the five, leaving Dell with $300.00 on the table.

They kept betting for hours.

Around midnight Dell hit a winning streak. He made fourteen passes and was beside himself with happiness. He kept playing, betting and winning the house money until he was up by fifty thousand. Incredible! He cashed out and headed to the roulette table.

Only one or two more plays there and he'd quit. Only he didn't.

The wheel kept going against him--red when he bet black, then black when he bet red. By two a.m. he was down to twenty-six thousand. Surely, his luck would change.

At five a.m. he left the casino with a hundred and thirty-six dollars.

Chapter Seventeen

At dusk on the ninth day of September April felt the first labor pains. She reached for her cell phone and called John.

"John, can you come now?" she asked.

"Labor?" he asked.

"Yes. I'll call Dr. Wesley."

"I'll be there soon as I can drive over." He sounded alert and excited.

"Meet me at the side door," she said.

"Fine. I'll be there," he said.

She gathered up the small bag she'd prepared and left her room. On the way down the stairs she called to Mary Jean who appeared from the kitchen.

"I'm going to the hospital now. It's time," April said.

"I hope everything goes perfect," Mary Jean said. "Anything I can do?"

"No, except don't tell anyone where I am. Especially, don't tell the captain if he should call."

"What do you want me to say?" Mary Jean asked.

April frowned. "Maybe try to dodge the question by saying 'why don't you check at the store?' Actually, the staff there does not know where I'll be."

"But if that don't work?"

April held her stomach and moaned.

"Oh, a pain," Mary Jean said. "Maybe you better sit down."

April slipped into a nearby chair. In a few minutes the pain eased away.

Almost immediately, John arrived and Mary Jean answered the door. He greeted her briefly then went to April.

"How are you?" he asked, touching her shoulder. He appeared concerned.

"All right so far," April said. She turned to Mary Jean, "If pressed to say where I am, say it's not your job to know, but maybe you won't have to go that far." She paused and added. "But do let Jayson drive you anywhere you need to go."

"Don't worry," Mary Jean said. "I know what to say and what not to say. I can handle it."

April gave her a quick hug. "Thanks," she said.

April and John left then for the eighteen mile drive to Pioneer Community Hospital in Aberdeen. It was growing dark, and a light rain pelted the windshield.

Soon after they were on the highway April noticed an SUV appeared to be following them.

***

Faith Ann felt her relationship with Dell was somehow unfinished. She didn't want to go to his house and ring the doorbell, but she was curious about a few things. She drove by the front of Dell's house, and then down a little side road. She wanted to see what he'd done about the grove of pine trees. Not a single tree stood. How foolish not to consider the future! Dell really needed someone to force reality into his brain. Her mama would say "hold his feet to the fire."

She drove on into town hoping to run into him, as if it were an accident. She circled around for several blocks. Finally she was rewarded. There his car was, parked in front of the paint and hardware store. She drew up to the curb and parked two cars down. Then she sat and watched until she saw him leave the store. She slipped out of her car and called to him.

He stood waiting. "What?"

"Did you buy something to repair the dishwasher?" she asked.

"No, just some nails."

"Are you going to have the painting and repairs made?" she asked.

"Nope."

"Why not?"

"Waiting on my inheritance, but that's not your problem," he said.

Faith Ann flushed. "You threw away your pine tree money, didn't you? That's so stupid! I had hoped to help you, but I see you're never going to learn."

"I didn't ask for your help or your advice," he said.

"I'll say one thing. You sure lack whatever it was that drove your grandfather to build a fortune. Grow up!" She turned and ran back to her car.

On the way home she spoke aloud, "The unfinished business is finished, and I don't know why I care." Tears came. She had to admit she'd hoped for something much more from him. She'd already thought of how she'd change the draperies of his house; their house, in the parlor.

***

Mitchell Redmond opened the letter from Marlene with a knife. A knife turned out to be a fitting tool. Marlene wrote only one sentence. "I'm getting a divorce, and don't bother to send me anymore damned roses." She didn't even sign the note. Wow, he didn't expect that! She'd almost always been agreeable with few demands. Now what was he going to do? He couldn't have her making him look bad. He'd have to arrange a leave to go home and make up with her somehow.

In the meantime, he'd try to get through to her on the telephone. With caller ID she'd likely figure out he was the caller and not answer if he called from his usual number. He'd get around that. He'd use a pay phone. Maybe that would work. He went to the post bank and got six dollars in change, then found a pay phone near a gasoline station on the way into Columbus. He dialed his home number and got the answering machine. Probably she was out somewhere. He hoped she'd not gone to see a lawyer. He stood in the phone booth feeling frustrated. How could he get to her? Roses for sure didn't work. What was the most important thing in her life? The children! Of course, he'd go home and work from that angle. Even if she'd let the word out, he knew he could mend things and people would forget. In the meantime there was April, who had soured on him, too. Still, he had confidence he could win both of them back. After all, he knew both had adored him. And thinking of April, he decided to call her.

Again Mary Jean answered.

"May I speak with Mrs. Stembridge?" he asked.

"I'm sorry, she's not available."

"Is she at home?"

"Why do you ask?"

"I thought she might be available a little later...unless she's not at home."

"She don't want to receive any calls tonight," Mary Jean said.

"Has she already gone to bed? So early. Is she ill?"

"No, she's not ill."

"Has her baby been born yet?"

"You are asking so many questions, sir. Actually, no, but I'm busy so I must hang up now," Mary Jean said and promptly replaced the receiver.

He sat thoughtfully for a moment before placing a coin in the slot of the pay phone. Marlene answered this time.

"Darling," he began.

She cut him off. "Get lost!"

Mitchell sighed. He was tired and frustrated. He'd go back to the bachelor officer's quarters and figure out something tomorrow. Women! So temperamental! But this was all temporary. He'd win them back with his good looks and charm. It was just a matter of time. Annoying, but temporary.

***

April told John they were being followed by someone in an SUV. She sounded frightened.

He reached to hold her hand, "I know. It's Mason Carter, a deputy from the department."

"How do you know?" she asked.

"He was assigned to keep watch at your home, to be sure you were safe. You certainly are observant. I didn't think you'd notice tonight."

"You didn't tell me," April said. "Why?"

"I didn't want to upset you, but we wanted to be sure you weren't bothered by the captain, or anyone, for that matter."

"Do you think I'm in danger?"

"I hope not, but I didn't want to take any chances," he said.

"You do think I'm in danger, or you'd not have gone to that extent...not just to keep me from being annoyed."

"I'm going to do whatever it takes to keep you from being annoyed and keep you safe if danger should arise."

"Oh, oh, oh!" she moaned.

"Pains?"

"Yes."

When the pains passed, she asked, "Why do you think I could be in danger?"

"I had hoped to discuss this later," he said, "but...and I could be wrong...sometimes when people want their way they can become forceful. The main thing is to keep you comfortable and safe regardless."

"I don't feel I'm in danger, but I appreciate your looking after me."

"I don't want you to worry, honey, but do be careful. If the captain shows up, I don't think you should let him in your house."

"I definitely will not, and I'm having Jayson go with me everywhere I go. I had already decided simply to keep from being annoyed."

"I think we've arrived," he said turning off onto another street.

"Yes, this is the street," April said. "The hospital is at 400 S. Chestnut Street."

"We're almost there, and Mason has escorted us all the way."

"Oh, that didn't seem necessary."

"Probably not," he said.

"I didn't call my parents. I didn't want Daddy to be driving now that he's not well, and he would insist," April said.

"I'll get in touch with them after the baby is born, and also go by to let Mary Jean and Jayson know."

***

At ten-thirty a.m. on the tenth of September, a nurse spoke to John in the waiting room. "You have a fine baby boy," she said. "You may go in now and see your wife and the baby."

John didn't bother to explain his relationship but followed the nurse through the doorway and down the hall to April's room. He went immediately to the bed and kissed April's forehead. "How are you?" he asked, gently stroking her hair.

"I'm fine. Look at Clarence Sean Stembridge. Isn't he beautiful?" She turned back the light blanket partially covering him.

"Beautiful? Handsome, I think, since he's a little boy," John said, smiling.

April said, "The nurse told me he weighs seven pounds and three ounces and is twenty-two inches long. I've checked, and he has all his fingers and toes and everything."

"Perfect! I suppose you'll need to be here a day or two," John said.

"I haven't been told, but you can't stay. Thank you so much for all you've done, but you must go home now and get some rest."

"I will as soon as Mason gets here. He slept last night, so he'll sit watch outside your door today."

"Really? Do you think that's necessary? I should be perfectly all right here in the hospital."

"I think so, but we're not taking any chances that you'll be bothered. I'll be back later, and the other deputy will be here tonight when I have to leave."

"Gee, total coverage! Needed or not, I appreciate it, John," she said and lifted her arms welcoming him to an embrace and a kiss.

When he was gone, April studied her baby. Would he have the typical Stembridge round blue eyes? It did not appear so. He was, by anyone's standards, a good looking newborn with regular features, blue eyes and soft brown curls. Did he resemble Mitchell? She couldn't tell. Maybe when he was a few days older it would be clearer who, if anyone she knew, he resembled. She remembered she had not taken her appearance from either of her parents. Would Sean look like some ancestor on either side of his family? She bent to kiss him. Already she loved him, regardless of who his father was.

April thought of Clarence and Claudine. She felt a certain peace, since she'd named Sean as Claudine had wished. There was a portrait of the distinguished grandfather, Sean William Stembridge, in the hallway of the mansion, but she'd never looked at it carefully. Now she would study his features. She hoped there would be a likeness, but as much as she wished otherwise, her little one might resemble Mitchell Redmond or his ancestors.

***

Every attempt Mitchell made by long distance to get back into his wife's good graces proved fruitless. Finally, he flew home.

He rented a car and arrived unannounced. His key no longer fit in the front door, and no one answered when he knocked. He walked around to the back of the house and came upon Marlene and the children in the yard gathering apples from their miniature fruit tree.

Sarah, who held a yellow apple in each hand, saw him first. She dropped the fruit and ran to meet him. "Daddy! Daddy!" she cried.

He swooped her up in his arms and kissed her cheek. "Daddy's girl!" He said.

By this time Warren had seen him and ran to throw his arms around Mitchell's legs. "You come home!" Warren cried.

Mitchell looked at Marlene. "Honey," he said, "you wouldn't tear up their world, would you?"

"Who tore it up? Certainly not I," she said. "Not I, the perfect political wife."

"Marlene, please! We have to work this out. I'm begging, honey."

"Our puppy, Squeezer, begs, Daddy," Warren said. "You want to see him?"

"Not now, Warren. Later." Mitchell looked across at Marlene, who had not moved from her position by the apple tree. "Let's, you and the kids and I go out to dinner. I don't have long to stay. Have to leave in the morning."

Marlene stood silent for a long moment biting her lip before she spoke. "Well, we'll do that, and you can sleep in the guest bedroom."

Mitchell felt he'd made a tiny inroad. "Thanks, honey. Believe me, I'll never hurt you again. Never, as long as we live, and I didn't mean to this time."

"We'll go to The Chicken Roost. The kids like it there."

***

Later that evening, back home, Mitchell asked, "Are you sure you want me to sleep in the guest bedroom?"

"Yes," she said.

Dutifully, he went to bed in the guest bedroom, but early in the morning, he walked quietly down the hall and slipped into Marlene's bed. She turned in a half wakeful sleep and he took her in his arms. Now more alert she pushed him away, but not forcefully.

"Don't," he whispered.

She allowed him to hold her but tears ran down her cheeks. He kissed her and dried her tears gently with the edge of the sheet.

"I love you, Marlene," he said. "I'll always love you." He kissed her face softly and then full on her lips.

"Oh, Mitch," she cried.

"Please, forgive me," he said.

She responded then with passion. Ah, he thought, now everything is all right.

He lay back on his pillow. But what would happen if he brought the baby home? Maybe he'd better get April to give him a generous payoff to leave her alone. Of course, he could promise no more demands, but once she agreed, the cash could continue to flow indefinitely. That could be the best plan.

Marlene rose and went to the bathroom. "I'll make breakfast. Blueberry pancakes."

"Great," he said. "love 'em. I'll come help, so we can spend the time together."

She looked back with a smile.

Yes, everything was back on even keel. Good thing he'd made the trip.

***

John drove April and the baby home from the hospital two days later. Jayson had already picked up her parents, so they met their grandchild for the first time.

Flaudie Mae's face glowed with happiness at seeing her grandson. She took him from April's arms and cuddled him.

Marvelous said. "He looks good all right, but I hate being an old grandpa."

"You'd be the same age, grandpa or not," Flaudie Mae said. "He's just precious and so beautiful! Look at that sweet face and that curly hair. I don't know who he looks like, but he's wonderful."

"Mother, Daddy, this is Detective John Kelly. You remember him," April said.

"Yes," Flaudie Mae said. "It's so nice to see you again, Detective. Thank you so much for helping April."

"My pleasure," John said.

"You her boyfriend?" Marvelous asked. "I thought it was a captain somebody."

"It's not a captain anybody, Daddy. And yes, Detective Kelly is my friend."

"Boyfriend?" Marvelous persisted.

April and John exchanged glances and smiles.

"Yes," she said.

***

Acting upon Mitchell's instructions, Aero telephoned April in the afternoon when Sean was a week old.

"April, this is Aero. I think you liked Helen. Did you hear she had a heart attack and died?"

"Yes, Aero. I read it in the paper. I'm so sorry. She was a thoughtful, nice person," April said.

"She sure was. I miss her. How are you? I haven't seen you in a long time."

"I'm fine, thank you. How are you, Aero, other than missing Helen?"

"Aw, I'm pretty miserable. I just can't seem to be happy, but that's not your concern. Did you have your baby yet?"

"Yes. I have a fine little boy."

"Do you reckon I could stop by and see him sometime, and you, of course?"

"You're not thinking of coming with Mitchell are you?" she asked.

"No, just me."

April hesitated, but then she had an idea that she might get some important information from him without his really realizing it. "Yes," she said, "you could come alone. Just you, you understand."

"Yes, just me. I understand," He said, "How about later this afternoon before I go to work?"

"Let's see. You go in to Hector's at five thirty or six, don't you?"

"Six now."

"Well, come by around four-thirty if that would suit your schedule," she said.

"Fine. Yes, I'll be there," he said.

***

Dell was desperate for money. He scraped through Grandma Stembridge's jewelry box and found the few remaining gold pieces, which he took to a pawnshop. Thirty-one dollars for two worn-thin rings and a broken gold bracelet. It seemed too little, but at least it was something.

On the way home he passed a line of oak trees where acorns had dropped onto the sidewalk. He crushed them as he walked, trying to think of how to come up with more cash. He couldn't think of a single other thing he could take to the pawnshop. He searched his mind as he walked, selecting acorns to crush...crunch, crunch, crunch.

Then it came to him! That antique Estey Pump Organ he'd never use. He'd get April to buy it. Yes, that's what he'd do. It must be worth at least a thousand dollars. But what if she wouldn't buy it? Probably say he'd just gamble the money away. Step, step, crunch, crunch.

He sighed deeply. No way she'd buy anything from him, believing he'd gamble it away unless...unless he made up with Faith Ann. Dang, he didn't want to do that because Faith Ann would want to plan how the money would be spent.

Still, if April liked Faith Ann, and she was practically guaranteed to like her, it could work. April might be convinced he'd given up gambling because of Faith Ann and because of his last lousy gambling experience. Yeah, he could play that up, that change of heart thing, after the loss of his pine tree money. Sure, that would work. He kicked the acorns off the walk on either side in a little scuffle.

Problem. Would Faith Ann accept him again? Maybe she would if he took her a little gift, hung his head and said he was sorry...yeah, she had really liked him a lot. But better not spend any of his thirty-one bucks on a present. Maybe he could find some little trinket at home...something else left of Grandma's. He'd take another look in her jewelry box when he got home. Nothing expensive. Maybe some little glass beads.

Immediately after he reached home he ran up the stairs to Grandma's bedroom and checked her jewelry box. Not much in there. He'd long since pawned the best pieces and never got them back. He stirred the items around. A cameo. Hey, that might bring a few bucks. Some broken earrings. He closed the top drawer and pulled out the second drawer. There! That would do, a strand of yellow glass beads, with a teardrop and a gold, or maybe just gold colored clip. He searched around on top of

Grandma's dresser for a box. There...a little wooden box with some carving on it. Yeah, that would do fine. He dropped the beads into the box, but then added a dingy square of cotton from a paper carton. Good. Faith Ann would probably be touched, even thrilled. He glanced in the dusty mirror and brushed his hair in place with his hands. Now, off to the Burger Castle and hope she'd be working today.

Chapter Eighteen

The chief and Kelly were sipping coffee at two o'clock in the afternoon in the chief's office. It was September seventeenth, almost ten months to the day since Clarence Stembridge's murder. Kelly was frustrated. Clues surfaced here and there but nothing concrete.

"Chief," Kelly said, "this is taking much longer than I had hoped. No overturned rock has turned up the worm, as you know. I'd hoped for an arrest by now."

"You've covered a lot of bases, John. Try not to get discouraged. Have you questioned all of the suspects on the list?"

"Not all. For one thing, I've never been able to connect with Mitchell Redmond. He's away on temporary duty or home on leave. I think, though, I may be able to catch up with him at Hector's this evening. I'm driving out there early this afternoon and waiting to see if he shows up."

"Good idea, John," the chief said.

"Never have had a direct contact with Aero Laston either, although I talked with his girl friend about him before she died."

"I remember. The guy sounds like he's off his rocker."

"Yes, he's been in the mental hospital, but he's out and back working at Hector's." Kelly said. He rose from his chair and prepared to leave. "I might be able to interrogate both of them tonight. Think I'll see if I can nail Laston first. He'll probably go to work before Redmond shows up."

"Seems in a good order anyway, as he's likely not as sharp as Redmond. Might let something slip that Redmond wouldn't."

"I'm on my way. Talk with you later," Kelly said. He reached into his pocket for his car keys and left the chief's office.

When he reached his car, Kelly called April on his cell phone. "How're you today and how is Sean?" he asked.

"Fine. We're both doing well," April said.

"Any problem?"

"No."

"How about the captain?"

"No. His friend, body guard type, is coming by to see the baby and me today."

"That guy Aero?"

"Yes. I liked his girl friend and Aero has always been nice to me," April said.

"He's too close to Redmond for my comfort. I don't like him visiting you," Kelly said. "What time is he due?"

"Around four-thirty. He said he has to be at work at six o'clock but he won't be here very long. I don't think there's a problem, John. He knows he's to come alone. I kinda think he wants to cry on my shoulder about the loss of his girl friend. He knows Helen and I liked each other."

"Don't be too trusting, Honey. I'll send one of the deputies over. You can let Henry hide out of sight, but be available just in case."

"Oh, John, I don't think that's necessary."

"Indulge me," he said.

She sighed. "Well, all right. I don't mean to be difficult. I appreciate your help. I really do."

"Like I said, I'm going to look after you," he said. "I'll call you later this evening."

"Fine. Thanks again."

As soon as Kelly hung up from talking with April, he called Deputy Carl Henry and explained the need for a watch. "Can you get away to go over there now?" he asked.

"Sure can," Henry said. "I'll take care of it."

"Good. April thinks there's no problem, but she could be too trusting. This guy is very unstable...you may remember he's been into drugs and in the psychiatric hospital. He could be behaving normally now, but I just want to be on the safe side," Kelly said.

"I understand. I'll get right on over there and get positioned out of sight where I can hear everything."

"Good. We'll talk later," Kelly said.

"I'll call you after the guy leaves," Henry said.

"I better call you instead. Say sometime after six p.m."

"Okay."

***

Two weeks after Aero moved into Helen's house, he and Mitchell were seated in her small den talking. Nothing much was changed except Aero had put pictures of her on the wall and on the mantel. At night he always kissed the picture of her on the bedside table before going to sleep.

Today, however, Helen was not being discussed. April was. After overhearing Aero's telephone conversation with April, Mitchell clapped Aero on the back. "Good job!" he said. "Now you know what you're supposed to do. Don't mess up. No drinking. No drugs."

"I need a little something for my nerves," Aero said.

"One drink. That's all." Mitchell continued, "On this first visit, Aero, I want you to be very nice. Don't in any way show any intention of anything except to have a pleasant visit. Take a good look at the baby to see if he bears a resemblance to me. Got that?"

"Yeah, I can do that. It's the next visit I'm worried about."

"Now don't go jumping ahead! This visit is a first step. April may have a recorder on, so don't say anything at all suspicious. Got that?"

"Yes. Like I said it's the next time I'm worried about."

"Aero, it may take several steps and different plans, but today, just be as lovable as possible. You like April. Remember? She likes you. Be complimentary and keep your voice soft. Talk some about Helen. Cry if you want to. The point is to make her comfortable and trusting. Got it now?"

"Yes." Aero sat with his head down.

"Quit worrying about next time. Next time you're going to take a present for the baby. Today you'll say you didn't have time to buy a gift but you'd like to drop a present off sometime next week if that's okay."

"But next time is going to be hard," Aero said. "You want me to do something I can't do. I can't swab that baby's mouth with April right there."

"Find a way so I can have it tested for the DNA. Hell, man, think! Ask her for a drink of water so she has to leave the room. Anything to have the chance, and be damn careful that Mary Jane or Jayson won't see you. The nursery is probably close by where you and April would be sitting. Oh, I don't know, but find a way."

"I can't," Aero said.

"Yes, you can. If you can't do it on the second visit...do it on the third. Damn, Aero do I have to do all your thinking?"

"I don't like it. I really don't think I can do it."

Mitchell raised his voice, "You can and you will or we're through. Got that?"

Aero glanced at Mitchell and swallowed. "I didn't mean I wouldn't try."

Mitchell softened his voice to almost a whisper. "Get it done, Aero, or the police will know more about you than you want them to know. That, big buddy, can get your ass fried. Think, Aero. Compare prison, plus possibly the hot seat, to the great surprise I have for you if you finish the job."

"It's time to go," Aero said. "Give me a shot of Old Charter."

Mitchell poured him half a glass of the whiskey.

"More," Aero said.

"No. You're not going in drunk."

***

Dell drove his Cadillac to the gas station and put in ten dollars worth of gas, then he went to the Burger Castle to try to see Faith Ann. When he went in he didn't see her.

"Where is she?" he asked.

"Went downtown to look for a better job, I think." A petite, freckle-faced girl said, "but she might not. She might be at home."

"And where is home?" Dell asked.

"On Crying Willow Road. A little white house with a picket fence. You'll see it around a bend."

"Crying Willow Road?"

"Oh, no," the girl laughed. "It's Weeping Willow Road."

"I know where that is," Dell said. He smacked the counter with his hand. "I'm off," he said.

In less than ten minutes he found the place. He noted the perfectly painted small white house and the neat picket fence. An old house in an old neighborhood, apparently retouched with Faith Ann's brush. He saw the house sat ever so slightly tilted on the well-kept yard. He was certain Faith Ann would have straightened the tilt if at all possible. He smiled. A frustration for Little Miss Perfect.

He punched the red button of the doorbell and waited. He had not seen her car, but it could be parked out back of the house. Again, he pressed the doorbell and this time he heard a thumping sound inside. A middle-aged woman with graying red hair opened the door. She was leaning on a walking stick.

"Yes?" she asked.

"Is Faith Ann in?" he asked.

"No, she went into town," the woman said. "Could I help you?"

"I'm Dell Stembridge, a friend," he said.

"Oh, well, she's mentioned you. Come on in. She should be back before too long. Went to a job interview. I'm her mother."

"I see the favor," Dell said. He entered and closed the door behind him. Inside he saw crisp, white ruffled curtains at the windows. The rocker and two armchairs were painted red, as was the wood on a day bed. By a window, a small table bore a vase of artificial white daises. All of the cushions in the room were brown, matching a worn rug covering most of a wide plank wooden floor.

"Could I get you a drink?" she asked. "I keep coffee on all the time and Faith Ann keeps lemonade in the refrigerator. So what will it be? Hot or cold?"

"Neither," Dell said. "I'm not thirsty."

"Have a seat," she said to him gesturing toward one of the armchairs near her.

A low fire burned in the narrow brick fireplace. Faith Ann's mother seated herself in the rocker and spread a white crocheted afghan over her lap, covering her knees.

Dell was surprised to see a fire in the fireplace. He'd not considered the early fall day chilly, but then he remembered Faith Ann had said her mother was not well.

"So what kind of job is Faith Ann applying for?" he asked.

"This home repair and construction company ran an ad," Mrs. Hogan said. "You know Faith Ann can do most anything, but they probably won't hire her. Chances are they're looking for a man, not a pretty young girl."

"Probably," Dell said.

"Now if her dad was still living, he'd have gone in with her and told them how smart she is and how he taught her to do building and repairs." She glanced at Dell. "Her dad wanted a house full of kids, but I could only have one. He made a boy and a girl out of her. Every Easter he bought her a beautiful dress. That was for the girl in her. Otherwise he pretty much taught her as a boy and sometimes called her F.A. or Junior. His initials were F.A., too...Frank Albert."

"I see," Dell said. He wished Faith Ann would return. It was much too warm in the room for him.

"Now if she can get that job, it'll pay a lot more than Burger Castle. She said if they turned her down, she was going to offer to work free for a week just to prove she could do the job. She's pretty determined. We'll see," Mrs. Hogan said. She glanced at Dell. "She said you was real good looking. I don't think so."

Dell flushed.

Mrs. Hogan laughed. "Ah, it runs in my family to joke. We joked about everything. Faith Ann calls my hand on it sometimes. Says it can hurt people's feelings, but it was the way my family was. Joke, joke, joke all the time. We 'specially liked the 'got ya' jokes. Nobody took it serious." She stopped laughing then and said, "No, actually, young man I think you look just fine, but you're awful quiet, so I just had to jar you up a little."

Dell said, "That's okay. Do you think she'll be back soon?"

"Don't have a stop watch on her. She may need to do some tall talking, but that's all I know."

Dell rose from his seat. "I think I'll check back later," he said.

"Whatever suits you," Mrs. Hogan said adjusting the afghan on her lap. "I'll tell her you came by."

Dell had no sooner walked out the front door than Faith Ann drove up. She apparently meant to park her car in the back, but she stopped by the fence when she saw him.

"Come get in," she called.

He bounced down the steps and rushed over to get into her car. "Did you get the job?" he asked.

"Yeah, sure did. This really nice young man hired me. His name is Paul Singleton. He's the son of the owner. It's Singleton's Construction. He said he'd just finished college, but he's older because he took a year off to travel and then he spent another year as a missionary to Peru where he helped build churches."

"So you got the job," Dell said. Maybe he should have brought the cameo to impress her more.

"I'm to start Monday at fifteen dollars an hour. Imagine! That sure beats minimum wage, and Paul said that was just during the three months trial period. After that it could go up."

"I brought you a little gift," Dell said, again interrupting her. Not that he cared about the spark of a possible romance with another man, but he needed her service. "Hey, and I'm sorry for what I said. I didn't mean it. You were so right about the gambling." He handed her the little wooden box.

"Oh, thanks," she said. She removed the beads from the box and put them on immediately. "These are so darling!" she said. Then she looked at the box. "A carving of the Eiffel Tower," she said and turned the box over. "Great! It's a music box. Script reads 'made in France 1895.' " She wound the tiny key and an unfamiliar but pleasant tune tinkled forth from a spinet.

Dell frowned. Damn! He hadn't realized it was an antique music box from France. He could have pawned it for a good price.

When the music stopped, Faith Ann reached over and kissed his cheek. "Thank you so much," she said, "Both are wonderful gifts. Amber beads are not only lovely. The gemstone is supposed to bring good luck."

He bit his tongue. He didn't think it was expensive jewelry. Whatever. It was hers now, and maybe it would pay off after all. He said, "Glad you like them." Better ask her now to go meet April. Now while she was pumped up over the gifts. She might not be available later. He opened his mouth to speak but was interrupted.

She said, "Dell, I noticed they're advertising for a sales associate at that classy men's store downtown. I think you should go in and apply right away. You know you need a job, and that would be a good beginning."

A job? That was the last thing he wanted, but what could he say?

Faith Ann didn't wait for an answer. "Listen," she said, "I'll go in and tell Mama the good news, then I'll go with you to apply. Go on to your car now. I'll be with you shortly."

Dell got out of her car and walked to his. All right, he'd apply for the damn job. Then it occurred to him, it was not a bad idea. Yeah, he would apply for the job and take it if offered, then he'd drive with Faith Ann over to see April. Sure, that would make him look good. With that news in her ears, April would practically be guaranteed to buy the pump organ.

He snapped his fingers remembering. Doggone it! If he'd noticed that was an antique music box from France, he'd have pawned it. Well, too late now.

***

Dell and Faith Ann entered Clark and Major's stylish clothing establishment. *Fine Apparel for Men* was their slogan. A tall, elegantly dressed man with graying temples, greeted them.

"I uh... ." Dell stammered.

Faith Ann said, "He wants to apply for your opening as a sales associate."

The man frowned, looked at Dell and asked, "Yes?"

"I do," Dell said. "You see, I have no experience, so I was a little hesitant. I have a year of college and well, I think I could do it."

"He's Dell Stembridge," Faith Ann said. "You probably knew his cousins at Stembridge Antiques."

The man's frown changed to a cordial smile. "Yes, of course. Well, let's go into my office and talk over a few things. Oh, my name is Brandley, Harvey Brandley. I'm the manager."

An hour and forty-five minutes later Faith Ann and Dell left Clark and Major's with Dell employed. He was to experience his first ever job at age twenty three. Faith Ann patted his arm, smiled and congratulated him as they walked to the car.

Dell liked the fine Italian suit with all the accessories he was to wear on the job. He had to dress the part, and he'd admitted his wardrobe needed updating. When they reached his car, he placed the box in the trunk. Certainly didn't want some thief to rip it off. He thought the manager amazingly trusting to have made such a generous advance, but he realized the Stembridge name carried weight. Maybe he wouldn't have to work hard.

***

Dell and Faith Ann arrived at April's home as Aero was leaving. Introductions were made all around.

Aero extended his hand for a handshake with Dell who responded. "Believe I've seen you at Dugger's fights."

"Yes, I've been a few times," Aero said.

"Guys keep showing up to fight him, but no opponent ever wins," Dell said.

"He's tough," Aero agreed. "Well, I have to leave for work. Good meeting you folks."

"Nice to meet you," Faith Ann said. She smiled at both Aero and April.

Minutes later, Aero got in his beat up old black Ford and drove off. The smelly smoke from his faulty exhaust filled the air, causing the others to frown and rub their noses as they turned to enter the house.

April spoke to Faith Ann. "I've heard nice things about you."

"Really? A compliment is nice. Thanks for telling me." Faith Ann beamed and glanced at Dell, who appeared preoccupied.

"I hear your baby has arrived," Dell said.

"Yes. Clarence Sean Stembridge is a week old now. Come in and meet him." April said.

Dell and Faith Ann followed April into the house and upstairs to the nursery. Sean was awake looking around, kicking his feet and waving his arms in the uncoordinated way of a newborn.

Faith Ann said, "He's beautiful! Honest! I wouldn't say that if it weren't true."

April smiled. "Thanks."

Dell studied the baby for a long moment. "Sure is," he said, but April noted his facial expression changed from neutral to a frown. She thought he probably was surprised to see the baby's eyes were not round, but almond shaped.

April said, "Do you know of anyone he resembles, Dell? Perhaps the female side of the family."

"No, I don't see any favor, but he's a good one," Dell said.

April said, "Well, it's no big deal. I didn't look like my parents or anyone in the family when I was born, either. Of course, we can inherit from ancestors we may never have seen."

"True," Faith Ann said, "but I look a lot like my father with my black hair and dark eyes. Mother's a redhead with blue eyes. I was told dark is dominant."

"Yes," Dell said, "and some family characteristics you see over and over again."

April realized his comment was pointed, but she said, "Let's go in the den. Would you like something to drink?"

"Scotch and Soda," Dell said.

"I'm sorry. I meant soft drinks. I don't have anything with alcohol."

"Whatever then," he said.

"I'd like some ice water, please," Faith Ann said.

When April left the room, Faith Ann said, "She's so pretty and very nice. I'm glad you brought me to meet her."

"Yes, them good looks is what won her my cousin," Dell said.

"You don't sound as if you like her very much."

"Why would you say that?" he asked. "I like her just fine. She's going to give me a settlement on my inheritance I missed out on."

April returned with the drinks and handed them to her guests.

Dell said, "I want to sell Grandma's old pump organ. You reckon you'd be interested? I don't need it."

"An antique of course. I'll get Marvin at the store to take a look at it and give you a price," April said. "You're not going to gamble the money away, I hope."

"Oh, no. I learned my lesson the last time. Besides, as I told you, Faith Ann is not into gambling. She's helping me fix up the old home place." He then added in detail how clever Faith Ann had proven to be and told April about her new job.

"That's very impressive," April said.

"He has a job, too," Faith Ann said. "Tell her, Dell."

"Oh, it's just working at Clark and Major's."

April looked surprised, then smiled. "Good for you, Dell. You should do well there. I'm glad you've decided to count on something besides gambling."

When they were leaving, April said, "I think I'd like to have your grandmother's pump organ myself, Dell. At some time in the future, Sean might prize it as something from his great grandmother. I'll call Marvin about it."

Dell smiled. "Can he come take a look tomorrow?"

"I'll check. He'll call you," April said.

They left then with Dell holding Faith Ann's hand as they walked away.

Dell smiled all the way to the car but said nothing.

"What are you thinking?" Faith Ann asked.

"Just feeling like things are going my way," he said.

"Like what?"

"I don't want to talk about it," he said.

"A secret?"

"Yeah, you might say that."

Chapter Nineteen

Kelly waited at Hector's for Aero to show up. He was rewarded for his wait at five forty when he saw Aero leaving his car. Kelly left his car and approached Aero. He presented his credentials. "Detective Kelly, Mr. Laston, I need to talk with you."

Aero's eyes widened. "Me? Why?"

"Routine questioning," Kelly said.

"I have to be to work in a few minutes," Aero said.

"Sir, this takes precedence. If it gets long, we'll schedule another time to meet. Suppose we step up on the porch and sit in those chairs."

"Yes, sir, we can do that."

When they were seated, Kelly asked, "Where were you on the evening of November 19?"

Aero shook his head. "I have to tell you, detective, I have no idea. You see, I have this really bad memory for times and places. Probably goes back to when I was a boxer and got my brains knocked around." He was sweating and he kept brushing his hair back from his face.

"Are you saying you have no memory for any times and places?" Kelly asked.

"No. I remember Christmas and New Year's, but ask me where I was on any other date and I won't know."

"How about your girl friend's birthday?"

"Nope, not unless she's just told me a day or two before and even then I might forget."

"Helen Madison said you told her you were going to the doctor on the date you were to celebrate her birthday. Did you tell her that?"

"I might have if I didn't have the money to take her out. Sometimes I get real short on money."

"But you didn't go to the doctor."

"No. Well, I've seen a head doctor, but that's all," Aero said.

"You do remember telling Miss Madison you were going to see the doctor?"

"No, but I probably did. I'll say this, if Helen said I did, I did. She was right up front with the truth. I sure do miss her."

"The record shows you killed a man in the boxing ring," Kelly said.

"I did that. He hit me below the belt and made me so mad I just kept beating him and one lick was too much. Don't know why, but that's what I was told. Anyway, I quit boxing right then and there. I don't like killing. It's a bad thing."

"You don't like killing. Have you killed or tried to kill anyone else?" Kelly asked.

"Sir, it would take a mighty powerful thing to lead me to killing. Killing is bad."

"Are you saying you have not killed anyone else?"

"If I did, I'd have been out of my mind. Innocent by reason of being crazy they call it."

"But have you?"

"Well, if I was crazy and did it, I wouldn't remember, would I?"

"I think you're evading the question, Mr. Laston. Maybe I'd better take you downtown for more in-depth interrogation."

Aero paled. Mitchell would be furious! "No," Aero said, "I'm not a killer. I wouldn't do that on purpose."

"So you're saying you haven't killed anyone."

"Just that boxer, Carl Transfield, and I didn't mean to do that. Meant to beat him up, but not to kill him."

"For now, we'll end our talk," Kelly said, "but I'll see you again later."

Aero got up quickly. "Gotta get to work," he said.

When Aero was inside the building, Kelly called Deputy Henry. "What happened with the visit?" Kelly asked.

Henry said, "Aero was apparently nervous, but he was kind and certainly in no way threatened April. Don't know why he seemed anxious. Maybe that's just the way he is."

"Yes," Kelly said, "he's had psychiatric treatment. But he revealed no hostile feelings?"

"No. They talked like friends. He looked at the baby and praised him. Just a normal visit other than his quaking voice and trembling hands at times. He even wept briefly when his deceased girl friend was mentioned. Of course, April was very sympathetic and they parted on good terms. Oh, he did say he hadn't had time to buy the baby a gift and would return with one in about a week if that was okay with her. She said sure. That was all," Henry said.

"Another visit?" Kelly said. "I don't like the idea. We probably need to still keep a watch."

"Probably," Henry said, "the guy is not quite right somehow."

"I'll let you go now. See you later. Thanks for the report," Kelly said.

***

Kelly was making notes when Mitchell Redmond drove into his reserved parking space and got out of his shiny, black Mercedes. He was sharply dressed in uniform. Kelly knew some women were attracted to men in uniform and Redmond was movie-star handsome. Kelly thought, *this guy can wow the women and take his pick.*

In short order Kelly had Redmond's attention, and again he proceeded to do an interrogation on Hector's porch. By now it was twilight, and soft burning lights came on in the ceiling all around the porch.

"Captain," Kelly said, "I understand you know Mrs. Stembridge, the former April Johnson."

"Yes, but why do you ask?"

"You undoubtedly are aware that her husband was murdered the evening of November the 19 of last year."

"I heard about it," Redmond said.

"Where were you that evening, Captain?"

Redmond did not answer immediately. He looked down, then out toward the street. He seemed to be considering what he should say.

"A problem, Captain?" Kelly asked.

"Well, yes. I was with April. We continued our relationship after she married, but hey, I didn't kill her husband."

"Would she be able to verify she was with you on that evening?"

"She could, or you could check with the motel. Their records will show I was registered there on that date."

"So you continued your relationship after she was married. Did she know you were married?" Kelly asked.

Redmond did not meet Kelly's gaze when he answered. "I don't know. I don't think it mattered. You know, women today don't care whether or not you're married if they want to be with you."

"But did you tell her? You know she was only nineteen and from the country. Maybe pretty innocent or naïve at the time," Kelly said.

"Maybe so, but she's much smarter than you think. That was one of the reasons I enjoyed her company. Another woman I met was great looking, but there was no conversation in her. Pretty, but dumb as a rock when she opened her mouth. Stupid women bore me."

"Well, then, did you consider a permanent relationship with April? Divorce and re-marriage?"

Redmond said, "It crossed my mind, but not for long. I have a beautiful wife and two great kids. Marlene's just the wife I need for the long run."

"You possibly know Mrs. Stembridge has a baby. Do you think he might be your son?"

"I don't know. If he is, I'd want to be in his life."

"Have you asked her about that?"

"Yes, but she's not interested...now that she's settled in with the Stembridge name and riches."

"Have you considered pursuing the matter legally?"

"I thought of it, but I decided to honor her feelings. She wants me out of the picture," he said.

"That's probably a good idea," Kelly said. "Whether he's yours or not, he'll have a good home, and, if you made an issue of it, you could lose your family in the process."

Redmond smiled. "For a while anyway. My wife is a strong woman. It would take work to win her back."

"But you think you could?"

He smiled. "Oh, yes. She wouldn't want to give me up permanently."

Kelly said, "You're pretty sure of yourself, I see."

"Experience has taught me to be," Redmond said. "I've always succeeded."

Kelly looked at him for a long moment, but withheld his opinion. He reached in his shirt pocket for his sunglasses, placed them on and stood. He didn't ask about Claudine's shooting. He already knew Redmond was out of town on temporary duty that week end.

"That's all for now, Captain," Kelly said.

"For now? You still think you need to question me again? What for? I've told you all I know."

"I always keep my options open," Kelly said. He made his way down the steps and back to his car. Redmond stood watching him briefly, then entered the nightclub.

***

April was growing tired of Aero's visits. Every Wednesday afternoon for three weeks, he'd shown up around four-thirty. He was always well behaved, but he kept talking about Helen and in general appeared restless. April couldn't quite decide what to make of his visits other than his coming for her emotional support. She found it unpleasant to be around someone as anxious as he appeared. It was as if his unhealthy emotional state filled the room. However, she saw no need for the deputy to be there and requested that he stop coming and make other use of his time.

Aero always wanted something to consume. April thought he behaved now like a baby wanting to be nourished. Like wanting to be fed by a mother person. He ate the food with passion, almost sucking it in while smiling. She thought it was petty on her part, but she found it irritating. Nevertheless, some small sympathy within her allowed her to grant his wishes and be kind about it. She used the intercom to ask Mary Jean to fulfill his requests for a Coke or glass of juice with cookies.

On his most recent visit, however, he asked for a sandwich when Mary Jean had gone briefly to the supermarket. April considered having him wait, but changed her mind and went downstairs to make the sandwich for him. She discovered one in the refrigerator already made...a ham and cheese she'd turned down for veggie soup at lunch.

When April returned upstairs she saw Aero in the nursery standing by the baby's crib. "Don't wake him, Aero," she said.

He hesitated briefly before turning around and returning to April's sitting room.

"He's such a good looking baby," Aero said.

"I agree," she said and handed him the tray with the sandwich and a glass of fruit punch. His hand shook as he received it, almost causing the tray to drop.

"Are you all right?" she asked.

"Yes," he said. "I just get a little shakey sometimes when I'm hungry."

"Aero, I'm planning to spend next week with my parents, so I won't be here for your visit," she said.

"Really? Well, have a good time. I'll see you later."

To her relief, he left as soon as he finished his food.

***

Mitchell was waiting back of Helen's house when Aero returned from his visit to April. He got out of his car and walked over to Mitchell's to report his near success in getting to swab the baby for the DNA. He didn't mention to Mitchell the fact that Sean was asleep, but admitted he couldn't get the job done, as April had reappeared so soon. He said, "I slid the paper and swab inside my shirt and buttoned it before I turned around."

"She didn't see that?"

"No, I had my back to her, and she was in the next room."

"Well," Mitchell said. "it's clear we need to know when Mary Jean will be away. Do you have any idea? As long as she's there, April will use the intercom."

"Right, but I don't know when Mary Jean will be gone."

"Find out. That's when you'll have your best chance. Then April will go get your food herself. Ask for something more like a sandwich with extra pickles, some chips and a soft drink with ice. Maybe also ask for three chocolate chip cookies. Or ask for pizza that will have to be put in the microwave."

"I'll see what I can do," Aero said. "Last week as I was leaving I saw Mary Jean sitting in a chair in the sun room near the side door knitting baby booties. I thought she was making them for Sean, but she said they was for babies at her church."

"Ah, so she goes to church," Redmond said. "Which church? When?"

"Don't know. I'll ask next time I'm there."

Redmond rubbed his hands together and smiled. "It's going to work out. Just taking a little time. You think the baby looks like me? With the right information in hand I can trump April's card, and the money will flow."

Chapter Twenty

Dell was pleased with the sale of the Espey organ, but the generous two thousand dollars April approved for payment to him would not last long. Certainly not now that Faith Ann was into repairs and painting again. It was frustrating.

With Faith Ann's new job she was not often as available. She was beginning to date Paul Singleton, and that also took time away from the work. If only he hadn't had to commit to repairing the house in April's presence! It was hunky-dory with him that Faith Ann and the builder's son were smiling at each other. Maybe Paul liked to be told what to do. Anyway, as soon she completed work on his place, Dell knew he'd be only too happy to say '*adios*' and hit the casinos.

If only he could get some real money! Ah, that was the rub, but he had an idea. If he could prove April's kid was not a Stembridge, he could pressure her for money to keep the secret.

He'd heard of court cases where DNA determined paternity. But how could he do that? He didn't know what he would need to do or even if he could legally get the information. He decided to telephone the library and ask if they had a book on it. No, maybe he'd just go to down there so he could get the information at once.

When he walked to the library Dell noticed the first touches of color in the trees, indicating fall on the way. Almost a year, and April kept holding off until the murder was solved. Too long. He wanted the money now. He felt well walking in the cool afternoon air, now that he had a possibility in mind.

It occurred to him to wonder if Clarence and Claudine would have accepted April if they knew the baby was not a Stembridge...was Claudine that desperate for someone to serve as an heir? Well, even if that was the case, April wouldn't want the public to know. Yeah, he had a chance if he could prove the baby was a bastard. In his eagerness he hastened his pace and soon was trotting along the old, cracked sidewalk. He was careful not to fall, although at one place roots had bucked the walk up in a slant. He stumbled, caught himself with his arm extended to the tree and rushed on.

At the library he asked at the desk about information on DNA tests and was referred to the computers. A young woman with fat cheeks and coke bottle glasses pointed him to the area.

"I don't know how to use a computer," Dell said.

"Oh, well, it's not hard," the librarian said. "I'll show you." She moved from behind the counter, and he saw she was pregnant. Well, gosh, maybe she knew something about DNA herself.

She slid onto a stool in front of a computer and soon pulled up information on DNA. "Here," she said, "you can read it or I'll print it out for you if you prefer."

"I guess you know about DNA," he said.

She smiled. "Yes, but I'm not the one wanting the information. Like I said, you may read it on the monitor or you can buy a print card for a dollar and print it out."

"I don't know how. Would you do that for me?" he asked.

"We don't normally provide that service, but okay." She shrugged and pushed the keys.

He fished in his pocket, brought out a dollar in change, handed it to her and waited while the document printed, and she handed it to him.

He smiled. "Good," he said and walked to a nearby table to sit and read the material.

He noted that he was instructed to read the entire instruction sheet before attempting to collect a sample. Okay, he noted, clean mouth. Rinse three times with warm water for the adult. For infants allow at least three hours past feeding, then allow the infant to drink room temperature water from a bottle.

Do not smoke/chew tobacco, etc. Well the kid wouldn't have done that. Skip on. The samples must be received by the lab no more than 5 days later.

Testing items may be procured from the lab or buy two sterile cotton-tipped swabs for each person at a pharmacy. A paper envelope is required for each person. Paper allows samples to stay dry. Do not use plastic!

Swab firmly on the inside of each cheek 30 times or about one minute. Thirty times. *April can't be anywhere around when I do this.* Allow swab to dry for ten minutes. Place swab in the envelope labeled with the individual's name.

Repeat the swabbing with the second swab. Seal the paper envelope and the first individual is finished.

He read, "you are not required to use the test participants' real names for this type test." Great! "Race and relationship required." Well, that's not a problem. Caucasian-- cousins.

"Use one mailing envelope size six by nine or larger. Print the name and address. Mail the envelope to the lab." Good! The cost? Wow! Two hundred dollars. He folded the paper and crammed it into his pocket.

***

Dell began to plan his visits to learn more about April's daily schedules. He learned that since she was often up during the night with Sean, she took her bath and a nap in the early afternoon. Good! He'd drop by for a visit hoping to find she'd just begun her bath.

He had the good fortune for that to happen. Mary Jean, who had become accustomed to his frequent visits, let him in to wait for April to finish her bath. Perfect! He was able to visit Sean and collect the sample. He cooed and was gentle in his swabbing to prevent Sean crying. When he'd accomplished his mission, he returned downstairs and told Mary Jean he remembered something he had to do, so he would leave and return another time.

***

In a conversation on his next visit, Aero learned that Mary Jean was a member of a Baptist church on the South side of town. Whenever possible she attended the early Sunday services at nine-thirty. She drove herself again to church most every Wednesday night around six-thirty and returned about two hours later, unless there was some special occasion. She invited Aero to visit her church, which she said was a mixed congregation of black, white and Hispanic members. She went on to tell him much more than he cared to hear about the programs and plans of the church.

"Does Mrs. Stembridge go?" Aero asked.

"No," Mary Jean said.

Aero said, "I just wondered if she was a church goer."

"She goes to her hometown church when she visits her parents."

"She's such a nice person," Aero said, "My girlfriend really liked her."

"Yes, she is," Mary Jean said. "Now you think about it and come visit our church. You could go with me if you liked."

"I would be at work on Wednesday nights," he said.

"That leaves Sunday. You'd be really welcome," she said.

"I suppose you see your family there. You're not married are you?" Aero asked.

"No, not married, but my family didn't want me, because I don't look to suit them. An old auntie raised me, but she's done gone to Heaven now."

Aero said, "You're sorta like my late girlfriend, Helen. She didn't have any family either."

"It's sad. I'd like to be with my family, but friends...really good friends can seem almost like family." She glanced at him.

"You seem to be kinda alone yourself. Where's your family?" she asked.

"Out of state. We didn't get along either. I ain't seen them in several years."

"Then you need friends, too. Do come to our church. Visit. See how you feel. I think you'll feel the love," she said.

"I'll think about it," he said. "I gotta go now. See you later." He left then quickly, eager to pass on the information to Mitchell. Doggone it, the girl touched him and he didn't want that. He didn't mean for that to happen. He just wanted the information, but somehow he got caught up in the conversation. Now he'd feel bad trying to slip in on a Sunday. It would feel like betraying Mary Jean...a person in a way like Helen. Well, it wouldn't be right away. April would still be off on her visit the next Sunday.

***

The wait for the DNA test results seemed endless to Dell. He left work to run home to check the mail every day at four o'clock. Bills and junk mail filled his box, but after seventeen days, on a Wednesday, the form arrived with the information. He ripped open the envelope and scanned the page in a glance.

Damn! The kid *is* his relative...a Stembridge, after all! He slammed the paper on the table and stamped around the room. Damn, damn, damn!

But then it occurred to him, he didn't have to *admit* the truth to April. He could say otherwise. Yeah! He could do that. She wouldn't know. He left then immediately and drove to her home. The beat up old black ford was out front. That Aero guy again. Okay, he'd not go upstairs, he'd speak to her just inside the door.

He rang the doorbell and Mary Jean answered. "Ask Mrs. Stembridge to come down here for a moment," he said.

"She has a visitor upstairs," Mary Jean said.

"I know, but I only need a moment of her time," Dell said.

"Very well, I'll tell her what you've said." Mary Jean left him at the door and he waited.

When she returned, she said, "She's tending the baby so you'll need to go where she is."

Dell snorted. He'd probably not be able to deal with the DNA plan, but he climbed the stairs and spoke to April and Aero.

"I'd like a word with Mrs. Stembridge in private," he said to Aero.

Aero blushed, but nodded his head and left the room. He walked into the hallway but lingered near the door. He was curious. What was so private? Was there a romance going on that Mitchell would want to know about?

Dell's voice carried well so there was no problem in hearing him. Aero thought he might as well have been in the room. Did the man not really care if he heard, or did he imagine Aero had gone out of earshot?

"April," Dell said, "I ran a DNA test on Sean. He's not a Stembridge, but you probably knew that."

"What?" April said.

"Your kid is not a Stembridge. I ran a DNA test."

"How dare you to do such a thing!"

"I thought from the beginning you wouldn't have hopped up to marry Clarence so soon if you hadn't had a problem."

"I want you to leave this minute! How hateful of you!" she cried.

Dell said, "I imagine you'd prefer this matter be kept secret. Why don't you just give me my inheritance money and we'll forget the test."

"Absolutely, not! Tell the whole world if you want to. Nobody will believe you, and if they should, they'd call you a sneaky, dirty rat!"

"Oh, I think the gossips will love it," Dell said.

"All right. You do what you wish. I can even move from this city if I choose to do so. Don't think you can force me to do anything Dell Stembridge!"

Out in the hallway, Aero was filled with mixed feelings. He had the DNA information to take to Mitchell but he felt sorry for Helen's friend. He slipped quietly down the stairs and left the house, *unaware he was leaving too soon.*

The conflict reached a pitch with April standing and demanding Dell leave immediately.

"April, April!" Dell said. "I was just joking. I admit I always thought of you as Little Miss Opportunity, and I kinda wanted to get back at you, but no, hey, look at this." He removed the DNA paper from his pocket and handed it to her. "He's ours," he said. "A Stembridge so everything is cool."

April could barely read the print for her tears. "Oh, Dell," she said, "I should kill you. Why did you have to lie to me?"

"I was mad at you and wanted to get a slap in. You know you keep holding back on my money. You say 'until the murder is solved'...which it ain't never gonna be. Otherwise, I simply wanted to know if Sean is family, and now we know he is."

"You were mean to be so sneaky, Dell. You thought I didn't love Clarence, but he was such a dear, sweet man, it was impossible not to love him."

"Do I still have to wait for the money?" Dell asked.

"Yes. I can't deal with it until the murder is solved."

"Trouble is, April, it won't be solved."

"You always say that, but you don't know. Besides, you have a job now, and Faith Ann has made improvements in your home. You can wait," she said.

"Just a small advance?"

She laughed. "You're impossible, you know. When the murder is solved and you're found innocent. And keep this in mind...a one-time gift. Period. So learn to manage money. Now go to your job and make big sales."

"Damn, April, I'm innocent. I didn't do it!" He stopped then and said, "Hey, the DNA test cost me two hundred dollars, a print fee and postage. How about a reimbursement on that?"

She went to her desk and took out her checkbook. "Two hundred and what?" she asked.

"Oh, make it two hundred and three dollars. I don't remember exactly."

She wrote the check, tore it out and handed it to him.

He smiled and tucked the slip of paper in his shirt pocket. Thanks was never in his vocabulary. He said, "Good girl!" and left bouncing down the stairs. That two hundred plus his salary check could add toward his next casino trip.

Chapter Twenty-One

Mitchell was waiting in his car behind Helen's house when Aero returned. Aero left his car and ran to the other vehicle, entering it quickly and closing the door.

"Mitchell," he said, "you're not going to believe this. I found out the baby is yours without having to do a thing but listen!"

"What?"

"Just let me tell you what happened," Aero said and he laid out the story in detail.

"Are you sure?" Redmond asked. "You're not just trying to get out of doing the job yourself."

"No. I could still do it, maybe next Sunday when Mary Jean goes to church, but Mitchell, I know what I heard. It was very plain. Besides, that baby looks like you. I told you that."

"All right. If you're completely sure, we're ready for the next step." Mitchell tapped his hand on the steering wheel.

"She wouldn't go for Dell's shakedown," Aero said. "She said she'd move out of town if necessary. Could be different with you, though. You probably can get the money."

Mitchell sighed. "I would've preferred it. I know we'd planned that as the next step and I'm surprised she'd take that attitude. I'm not sure I really believe she'd allow the public to know, but it could be true. She can well afford to move if she feels like it. But we'll go ahead with the final step."

"The final step?"

"Getting rid of April, of course. Otherwise, how do you imagine I can get the baby and his inheritance?"

"Maybe we should try the shake down first," Aero said.

"No. I've decided what you heard makes sense. If I were in her shoes and had all that money, I'd move...man would I ever move! I'd have other homes from ocean fronts to mountain places."

"She'd have to leave her store," Aero said.

"Like that's a big deal! She could move between her homes and return to Columbus whenever it pleased her. No, we're going for the final step. You can do it. She opens the door for you now and even feeds you."

"I can't kill her, Mitchell. I just can't do that."

Mitchell raised his voice. "You better if you know what's good for you, Aero. Must I keep reminding you of what will happen if your other crimes become police knowledge? Don't wimp out or you'll be dammed sorry, I promise you that, Buster." He stared Aero close in the face. "Do you want the rest of the story again?"

"No."

Mitchell smiled. "Remember the good part. Think...*only* this one last step...this final one thing to do and everything else will be great. I promise you."

Aero mumbled, "It wasn't so bad getting rid of him, but April... ." He sighed. "Well it *was* bad, but I kept reminding myself it was for you. I didn't want to do it, but I wanted so much to please you." He glanced at Mitchell. "Don't you see? That's how much I love you."

Mitchell said, "Stop that baloney! Clarence Stembridge was a big moron. He's better off. You did him a favor. Your lousy shot at Claudine missed, but we had help with that one. Maybe somebody was on our side."

Aero sat with his head down. "I did all that for nothing."

"Stop mumbling! You're not making sense. Now straighten up, go take a warm shower, get to bed and have a good night's sleep. We'll soon be in clover, Big Buddy." He laid his arm around Aero's shoulder, pulled him close and for the first time kissed his cheek.

Aero turned to face him with a hopeful questioning expression. Mitchell gave him a gentle shove. "Now get on with the plan," he said. "One more *little* thing you can do in a few minutes, Aero. Do it tomorrow. That's Wednesday isn't it?"

"Yes."

"All right. Come on to work after you finish and act natural. Hey, I'll give you a shot of Old Charter soon as you arrive at Hector's." He clapped Aero again on his back. "Later, Big Buddy."

Aero slid out of the car, closed the door and made his way toward what he'd started calling his home...his Helen house.

***

On their first real date, John came for April at seven o'clock on Tuesday evening. He was dressed in a dark blue blazer and gray slacks with a white shirt opened at the neck. April thought he looked more handsome than she'd ever seen him.

"I'm looking forward to this," April said. "I haven't been to The Fisherman's Catch in months. Their catfish is so good."

"It's one of my favorites. I like the view of the river from the porch. I asked for a reservation for seating there," he said, "I hope that's agreeable."

"Yes, I like that view myself," April said.

Mary Jean came up then. "Have a good time," she said, "and don't worry. I'll take good care of Sean."

"I know you will," April said, "but call me on my cell phone if you need me."

"Sure, if necessary, but I think everything will be fine."

They left then. Mary Jean set the security system and went upstairs to the nursery. She looked in on the sleeping Sean, then returned to the adjacent sitting room to read a magazine.

***

At the restaurant, John and April were seated on the porch with a view of the river as he had requested. Perhaps, on a Tuesday night a reservation wasn't necessary. They had the porch to themselves, and a waiter appeared promptly to take their order.

They found it relatively quiet with only soft music and the murmur of voices from inside the main area of the restaurant A full moon lit the dark waters enough that they could see small ripples, and at one point a john boat with one man drifted past.

"I like to fish sometimes when I can get away," John said. "How about you?"

"I've never been fishing, but I think I'd like it. I see us sitting on the bank of a creek watching the smooth water." She gestured 'smooth' with her hands. "We hope for a ripple, then we see a sudden running splash! We reel frantically and catch a big, wriggling big fish...like in the movies."

He laughed. "We'll give it a try sometime."

"Next spring. I like going out in nature on spring days."

"We'll do it," he said, "I know just the place."

They both grew silent for a long moment.

"I've never asked you," April said, "but how do you like being a detective? It must be hard work, but interesting."

"Yes, both, but I'm planning to go to law school next year, and then I hope to be a judge one day. I don't like the soft decisions some judges make today."

"Oh, you'll be a hanging judge then." She laughed.

"Well, maybe not always. What about you? You have your antique store, so you may prefer to stay home and raise your son."

"I've always been interested in art. I think I'll take a course to see if I have any talent. But whether I do or not, I'll enjoy trying to paint landscapes. Maybe I wouldn't have the talent to do faces, but that interests me. A person's face can say so much about what life has been to them."

"Yes, but not always," John said. "Criminal's appearances can sometimes be deceiving."

"You would know. I think, though, I'd choose simply on the basis of how interesting the face looked...good or bad."

"I have an idea you'll find you're more talented than you think." he said.

She smiled. "You know something, John, you're a really nice man. Not at all like I saw you when we first met."

"I was on another wavelength then, April. I didn't know you and I realized that although you appeared innocent, your surface appeal might be misleading."

She said, "That must be the detective in you."

"Plus a previous life experience," he said.

"Like what?"

He told her about his father and the young woman who took his inheritance.

"I see," April said, frowning.

"Forgive me, if I seem to be putting you in that position now. I know your decision was not the same...Claudine asked you to marry Clarence."

"She did, but I wasn't innocent. At the time, I was one scared to death country girl. I thought I could be pregnant by Mitchell Redmond, and he wouldn't marry me. Thank God, that didn't turn out to be the case! I have DNA papers proving Sean is a Stembridge. I simply can't tell you how much that means to me."

"You decided to get the DNA?

"I didn't." She told him how it happened.

"Dell really hoped to blackmail you, didn't he?"

"Yes. Dell is always desperate for money. I'll keep my promise to him, but he may eventually have to sell the old family mansion, and, because of his foolishness, even wind up on the streets. I'm sorry, but I'm only willing to give him a one-time generous gift if he proves to be innocent of the crimes. Enough is enough!"

"Try to talk him into counseling," John said, "but if he won't go, there's nothing more you can do."

Their catfish dinners arrived in platters with slaw and hush puppies. They looked at the appealing food and smiled across the table at each other.

"Smells so good!" April said.

"Ole Stackley knows how to cook it just right."

They ate then, hardly speaking for a few minutes. In the meantime, a family of four arrived and sat at a table near them. The family appeared in a good mood with adults and children exchanging light patter.

April said, "I like to see a family like that. Once I saw a father, at cafe, slap a little boy of about four, hard across his head several times and yell at him. I almost couldn't stand it. The woman and the little girl never said a thing. The child kept crying, and the man kept yelling. An elderly woman went to their table and asked if she could help. The man shouted at her to mind her damn own business. I've always worried about that child and wondered what happened to him."

"It can be a recipe for bringing up a criminal," John said.

"You know, John, I think sometimes the criminal behind the scene, like that cruel father, gets off scott free, while the child and the public pay. I'm for proper discipline, but definitely not abuse."

"Right, but sometimes parents who do a good job have kids go bad. Peer groups have a lot of influence."

"You'll make a good judge," she said.

When they'd finished their catfish, they ordered chocolate pecan pie. It came warm with a big roll of vanilla ice cream.

"Ah," John said at the end of the meal. "That was so satisfying. No beating an evening with a good meal in the company of a beautiful, smart lady."

"Such flattery." April laughed.

"In this case, it's not flattery," he said, "but people do love praise. Flattery, you've heard, will get you nowhere. I tell you, flattery will get you everywhere."

"With some people," she said.

"You're too clever."

She laughed. "I wish," she said.

When they left the restaurant, John asked, "Anywhere else you'd like to go?"

"No. I think I'd better go home now, but it's been delightful. Thank you."

They drove through the mostly dark streets of downtown Columbus back to April's mansion. When he opened the car door for April, she slipped into his arms and they kissed.

"Another blessing," he whispered and kissed her again.

***

Aero went to the bathroom, but not to shower. He reached for his razor. He'd have to punish himself in advance for April's murder. He dropped his pants and saw the deep scars he'd put there after killing Clarence. He hesitated, then hitched up his pants. Cutting was not enough. He turned and re-entered the bedroom mumbling to himself.

"I'm a worthless, no good bastard. Even as a kid nobody cared a shit for me. Well, Jimbo did a little bit, and what did I do? I picked on him and then I killed him. Killed Carl Transfield in the ring, killed Stembridge, then killed my Helen. Why in hell am I still living?"

He went to the desk in Helen's little writing nook where she did her correspondence and paid her bills. A drawer held plain, cheap stationery. He took out a sheet, picked up a pen, and sat motionless. Then he got up, went to the wall, and took down his favorite picture of Helen. With his pocketknife he loosened the brackets and removed the picture. He laid the empty frame down, slipped Helen's picture in under his shirt covering his chest. If only she could speak to him!

He returned to the desk and laid his head on his folded arms. What would Helen say? She'd say Mitchell Redmond was using him. She'd sure not want him to kill April. As always, she'd try to comfort him, try to make him feel better. For a moment, he relaxed, simply thinking of her calming voice.

He spoke to Helen then, holding his hand over his heart where her picture touched. "I'm not going to kill her, Helen. She was kinda gentle like you. I'm gonna turn myself in to the police. Well, not exactly. You watch. Maybe I'll see you later."

He took a pen in hand and began to write. He made three false starts, ripped the paper in shreds and began again. Finally he wrote out all his thoughts. Every detail. How he was a worthless nobody from birth. How he'd killed people. He made no excuse for the three accidental killings. He wrote how he loved Mitchell Redmond and how that love had caused him to kill for him. He spelled out the reason. Everything. All the details. How he was ordered to murder April, but couldn't. The gut spilling gave him relief, but he shook his head. It was too much. He still didn't want to hurt Mitchell, no matter what, and he didn't want to upset April. He tore the paper into small shreds, wadded it up and threw it in the waste paper can. Instead he wrote:

"To the police. I confess I killed Mr. Clarence Stembridge and shot Miss Claudine. I'm sorry. Aero Laston." He folded the sheet, put it in an envelope and addressed it "Police Office, Columbus, Mississippi." A stamp? Ah, there was a small roll of stamps in a corner of the drawer. He stuck one on the envelope.

Ready to go now, he stood, but then remembered something else. He sat at the desk again and took out another sheet of stationary. He wrote:

"This is my will. I want Miss Mary Jean Grearson, the maid of Mrs. April Stembridge, to have this house that was Miss Helen Madison's. I don't have anything else worth anything but one old car, but I want her to have everything that belongs to me. Please, don't mess this up, law people!! I really want her to have my property. Aero Laston, October 16, 2004." He felt good about that. Helen would agree. After all, Mary Jean was a little like her. He put the sheet in an envelope and held it in his hand. Who should he send it to? What if the wrong person got it? "I know," he said. "I'll mail it to April. She'll know what to do." He addressed and stamped the letter. Now he'd get to the post office and drop the letters in the mail. It was dark, and he had not eaten supper. Why eat? He was not hungry.

He turned off the lights and locked the door. Outside he smelled Helen's roses, now in late bloom. For a moment he considered cutting some to place on her grave, but he changed his mind. He got in his car and drove off down the hill to town. At the post office, he circled to the drop boxes and put both letters in before driving on to his old apartment building. Lights were on in only a few windows. The old building had lost most renters. That was good. He didn't want to be seen. His body likely wouldn't be found until morning, when he would be clearly dead.

He walked up the steps to the second level, where he'd once considered diving head first onto the pavement below. What if that wasn't enough? What if that didn't kill him? He went up another flight and finally to the fourth floor.

He stood for a moment looking down, then climbed over the rail and positioned himself for the jump. Within a minute he was going down-down-down...and then it was over.

***

Next day Aero's suicide was in the news everywhere: the television, newspaper and by word of mouth. Since his letter had not had time to reach the police department, no one knew why he had committed suicide.

John Kelly immediately began a search for more information. His first act was to secure Aero's residence. During his search, Kelly quickly discovered the shredded paper in the wastepaper can mixed with other trash. He passed the basket on to the special squad to piece the pages together.

"Wow, this will take a while, Detective," he was told.

***

In the meantime, Mitchell Redmond was furious when he heard the news. Still, it didn't appear, as far as he could tell, that Aero had involved him in any way.

Redmond paced the floor. The Stembridge goldmine was lost unless he could think of something. This was to have been the right time. Wednesday. It was already late in the day, and soon Mary Jean would be going to church. There was no way, however, that April would let him in the house...something that would have been no problem for that ape, Aero.

He continued to pace around the room muttering and shaking his head. "Damn! Damn! Damn! Damn him! Damn him to hell! Now what?" He stopped and plopped in a chair, holding his head in his hands.

Ah, but then an idea! If he could convince April he was somebody else! He rushed from the house to a department store and purchased female clothing "for my wife," he explained to the clerk.

He remembered April's actress friend who moved to California. He even recalled her name. Tracy Regal. April described her as a tall, beautiful girl, a scatterbrain, funny girl, who wanted to be "discovered" in Hollywood. He had hoped she'd return for a visit so he could seduce her.

Instead of going back to the Bachelor Officer's quarters, Mitchell rented a cheap motel room and dialed April's telephone number. He decided if she answered, he'd hang up. He wanted Mary Jean to answer.

He was in luck! Mary Jean answered on the first ring. He altered his voice to a high pitch and said, "Hi, I'm Tracy Regal, a friend of April's. I'm in town and want to drop by to see her for a few minutes. Will you tell her? I'm in a hurry, but I'll be there later. Thank you, dear."

Mary Jean frowned. Why didn't the woman ask to speak to April? She went upstairs and delivered the message.

"Oh, that Tracy!" April said. "She's such a scatterbrain. Did she say when she'd be here?"

"No, not exactly. Would you like me to stay? I don't have to go to church if you'd rather I be here."

"You seem uncomfortable," April said, "Why?"

"I don't know. She just sounded a little odd to me. Kind of a funny voice."

"Well, she *is* odd. No problem. You go on," April said.

***

Mitchell was pleased with his appearance when he finished dressing. He had no wig, but a floppy hat pulled down on his head with some of his hair for bangs seemed to work well enough for nighttime.

He poked a strong cord in his dress pocket. Small and fragile as April was it should be quick and easy...very quick and easy, right at the front door. It would be over in minutes and he'd be out of there! Nobody would know. Not even that deserting fool, Aero. Maybe this was better after all. Who knew what Aero would have blabbed later if he got stoned or drunk?

A glance at his watch revealed it was six thirty-five. Time to go. He locked the motel room where he'd left his uniform and made his way to his car. Better park a block away and walk. Someone could see his car too close to her mansion. At least Aero had done well in learning when the maid would be gone to church. Only April and his infant son would be there. He'd have to leave the baby, but not for long. Soon as the fuss was over about April's death, he'd show up and reveal he was Sean's father. Marlene would be mad as hell, but she'd get over it. He would always be able to work her.

When he approached the door it had been over two hours since he'd called, but April would be listening for the doorbell. He'd get her just inside the door. Fast work. Quick and easy.

Later Mary Jean would report the telephone call. The police would assume Tracy Regal was the big girl who did April in. Of course, that wouldn't last unless Tracy happened to be visiting in the old hometown. Hey, that would be good if she did happen to be in town. He laughed. There'd be no trace of his having been there. He tugged on his gloves.

Raising the hem of his long skirt, he rushed up the steps and rang the doorbell. As he had anticipated, April opened the door. He grabbed her and jerked the cord around her neck.

"AAAGH!" she tried to scream. She saw in his eyes that he meant to kill her. She shot her hand past his arms and clawed his eyes with her fingernails.

Gasping in shock and pain, he dropped the cord.

Momentarily blinded, he groped for her as she ran toward the spiral staircase. It occurred to her his long skirt could slow his climb.

She raced up the stairs, hoping Mary Jean had left the bottle of ammonia on the banister when she had cleaned. No! It was gone. Neat and orderly Mary Jean. Panting, struggling for breath, she reached the landing.

Initially, he stumbled over his long skirt, then held it higher and took the steps in long strides. He was within five steps of reaching her.

Where could she go? Thoughts flashed in her mind. Not the nursery! Not her bedroom! No time to reach the bathroom and lock the door!

Then she saw an opportunity.

He was looking down at the steps, holding up his skirt with both hands as he ran. More importantly, he was not using the banister. In a swift movement, she grabbed a straight chair, jammed it, legs forward, against him as he reached the next to last step. Blood ran from his cheek and he stumbled backward as the chair tumbled over him.

While he struggled to get up in his tangled dress, April ran down the stairs, into the kitchen. She'd no sooner closed the pantry door than she heard him cursing, running about looking for her.

***

At the police station, day workers had left, all except deputies Hazel and Jo Massey, twins, who continued to work diligently on sorting and piecing together the shredded letters Aero meant to destroy.

"What have you found?" Kelly asked, leaning over Hazel's thin shoulder as she placed another strip against the poster board.

"We have a way to go, Detective, but so far it seems this man is writing about his early life and his brother. Seems he wasn't loved and felt worthless."

Jo interrupted, "Here on my board he's talking about killing people."

"Jo, that's part of this letter. Here, let's get them together. See how these lines fit?"

"How much longer do you think it'll take to get it done?" Kelly asked.

"It was really slow go at first," Hazel said, "but we're getting there. I'm getting hungry. What time is it?"

"You're always hungry," Jo said. "It's six forty-three to the minute."

"Wait! Wait," Hazel said. "He mentions somebody named Mitchell Redmond wanting him to kill April...whoever April is."

Kelly jerked his cell phone from his pocket and dialed April's number. "Answer, answer," he whispered but there was no answer. He called across the office to Deputy Henry. "Have you checked the tap on April's phone?"

"No, but I'll do it right now." He listened to the recording and paled. "That's no woman's voice," he cried and recited the message.

"Let's go!" Kelly said. "Both of you." He swerved his arm to include both detectives. "Run!"

***

The front door of April's mansion stood slightly ajar when the police arrived, but they heard nothing. The stillness a frightening sound. Then, the opening of an inside door. Rustling sounds. A scream!

Where?

"This way!" Kelly yelled.

The men ran with Kelly in the lead. In the shadowy light of the kitchen they saw what appeared to be a big woman with her hands on the neck of a small person in shirt and slacks who kicked and struggled.

"Halt!" Kelly shouted. In an instant, the deputies flooded the kitchen with lights and action.

"Take him," Kelly yelled holding his pistol on the assailant.

"Oh, God!" April cried. "Thank you. Thank you. He meant to kill me!"

Redmond jerked and struggled against the detectives ripping the left underarm of his dress. "Damn bitch," he spat out.

"Shut up" the two detectives said in unison as they escorted him out the door.

John gathered April in his arms. She coughed and rubbed her neck. "How did you know?" April asked.

"I'll tell you all about it, but right now I'm reminded of something you said the other night at dinner. You said sometimes the criminal behind the scene gets away. True, but this one won't.

This page must be updated

If you do not use the internet, you may contact me to mail you a copy of any of my books. Also, I may eventually have each of them available at Faulkner's Antiques in Vernon. My telephone number is (901) 683-1115. If you have e-mail, my address is lgearin1115@bellsouth.net
Thanks! Louise *See attached page*   *P.242*

Books By Louise Murphy Gearin

Thicker Than Water *& Changes —*
When Rube's father learned Rube was a train robber he didn't approve, but he said he would support him because "Blood is thicker than water." At one point during the nineteenth century, Ruben Houston Burrow was the most wanted criminal in America. His family was unique, and the large Burrow clan did an incredible job of communication to keep Rube hidden when he visited home. The author owns the forestland where Rube's hideout cave is located. A true story told in creative non-fiction style.

An Unexpected Blessing
Belinda's adoptive parents are devoted to an evil cult leader who becomes a big problem for her when she reaches adolescence. Arson and murder occur as Belinda tries to find her way out. Fiction

Separate Paths, is a historical mainstream novel about Irish immigrants who come to America in a dangerous old wooden ship to escape starvation during the Potato Famine in Ireland, only to be met with The Five Points slum life, riots, cholera, and the Civil War. Two daughters are torn apart and live very different lives for years. You may call the toll free number to order this particular book (1-877-289-2665) when it is in print.* Fiction

Murderous Affections is a "who dunnit?" murder mystery set in Columbus, Mississippi. A wealthy antique dealer who appears to have no enemies is murdered. Who could possibly want to kill the unassuming, middle-aged man? Fiction

May 4, 2007 --

Murderous Affections is not yet in print, but should be within a month to six weeks.

*****Separate Paths** is not in print yet, but should be by the first of July.
All of the books should be available on Amazon.com and Barns and Noble.com by July.